Brett shot to his feet as the patio doors shattered, sending shards flying into the room...

"Get down, Anita," he shouted. But before he could shoot, his K-9, Mango, launched herself at the intruder and clamped down on the man's arm.

The man screamed, beating on Mango's head with his free hand. He dropped his gun and it clattered onto the floor.

Brett took a step in the intruder's direction, but suddenly a second man burst in, forcing him to confront the new attacker.

"Hold or I'll shoot," he said, but the man didn't seem to care—maybe because he was wearing armor on his upper body.

Brett didn't have that advantage and raced behind the kitchen island for protection, drawing the second man away from Anita as she huddled behind the couch.

Bullets slammed into the wood and quartz of the island, sending bits and chips of wood and countertop flying...

DANGER IN DADE

NEW YORK TIMES BESTSELLING AUTHOR
CARIDAD PIÑEIRO

INTRIGUE

To my amazing daughter and son-in-law, Sam and Dan.
Wishing you all the best on the addition of Axel Scott!
May he bring you immense joy!

Harlequin® INTRIGUE™

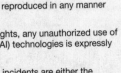

Recycling programs for this product may not exist in your area.

ISBN-13: 978-1-335-45712-7

Danger in Dade

Copyright © 2024 by Caridad Piñeiro Scordato

For questions and comments about the quality of this book, please contact us at CustomerService@Harlequin.com.

TM and ® are trademarks of Harlequin Enterprises ULC.

Harlequin Enterprises ULC
22 Adelaide St. West, 41st Floor
Toronto, Ontario M5H 4E3, Canada
www.Harlequin.com

Printed in Lithuania

MIX
Paper | Supporting responsible forestry
FSC® C021394

Visit the Author Profile page at Harlequin.com.

CAST OF CHARACTERS

Brett Madison—Brett Madison loved his time as a military policeman and small-town local policeman, but when his old friend Trey Gonzalez calls and offers him a position in a new K-9 security division, Brett jumps at the chance to work with South Beach Security and build a new life in Miami. He never expected his first assignment will reunite him with the woman who has haunted him for years.

Anita Reyes—Anita has worked hard to establish her restaurant on Miami's hot Ocean Drive in South Beach. Anita is dedicated to her business but also longs for time with her family and a second chance at love after a marine ghosted her years earlier and broke her heart.

Mango—Four-year-old pit bull Mango is a new addition to the South Beach Security K-9 division.

Ramon Gonzalez III (Trey)—Marine Trey Gonzalez once served Miami Beach as an undercover detective. Trey has since retired and is now the acting head of the SBS Agency and hoping to expand it with the addition of a K-9 division.

Mia Gonzalez—Trey's younger sister Mia runs a successful lifestyle and gossip blog and is invited to every important event in Miami.

Josefina (Sophie) and Robert Whitaker Jr.—Trey's cousins Sophie and Robert are genius tech gurus who work at SBS.

Ricardo Gonzalez (Ricky)—A trained psychologist, Ricky helps SBS with their domestic abuse cases and other civil kinds of assignments.

Chapter One

The pit bull nearly yanked Brett Madison's arm out of its socket as the dog jerked its head back and forth, thrashing forcefully, the pressure on his forearm punishing.

"*Pust*, Mango. *Pust*," Sara Hernandez commanded, and the dog instantly released his arm and sat, staring at him as if ready to attack again.

Sara strolled over and bent to rub Mango's head affectionately, ruffling her short, glossy white-and-tan fur. "Good girl, Mango. Good girl," she said and fed Mango a treat as Brett slipped off his baseball cap and wiped sweat from his forehead. Despite the mid-December weather that had brought a cooling breeze through the doors of the training ring building, the dog bite suit was hot thanks to its weight and padding.

"Do you think she's ready?" he asked Sara, the K-9 trainer who South Beach Security had hired nearly seven months earlier to run their new K-9 training center just outside Miami.

Sara smiled and chuckled. "Mango's ready. What about you?" she asked and shot him a look from the corner of her eye.

Brett dragged a hand through the short, damp strands of his high-and-tight cut and shook his head. "Possibly. It's only been three weeks that we've been working together."

"A solid three weeks and you've had a K-9 partner before," Sara said and skimmed a hand down his arm to reassure him.

"I worked with a K-9 during my time in the Marines, but

it's been a while," he said and rubbed Mango's head as well to reward the dog for her good behavior. It was while working as a military policeman that he'd met SBS acting chief Trey Gonzalez and then served with him during a second tour in Iraq. A tour that they'd both survived, although the scars remained.

"I think you and Mango will be happy together," Sara said and slipped the muscular dog another treat.

Brett unzipped the suit and slipped out of it. The cooler air bathed his sweat-drenched clothes, rousing goose bumps on his overheated skin. He rubbed his arms to wipe them away and then accepted Mango's leash as Sara handed it to him.

"You're ready," Sara said, reassuring him yet again.

"I am," he said and glanced down at Mango, who cocked her head to the side and peered at him with joyful cinnamon-brown eyes and a friendly grin, her tongue lolling out of her mouth.

"You are, too, Mango," he said, almost as if to convince himself. It had only been three weeks since Sara had paired him up with the pit bull and while the dog had performed amazingly well during their training, it would take more work and time together for him to feel as if he and Mango would be up for anything Trey Gonzalez might assign.

His friend Trey had reached out to him months earlier while he'd been working as a police officer in a sleepy North Carolina town. He'd liked the quiet at first after the trauma from his tour of duty but had been feeling lost and dissatisfied after several years.

When Trey had called with the opportunity to join him in Miami, he'd jumped on it. The fact that Trey now trusted him with one of the coveted positions in their new K-9 training program spoke to the fact that Trey was pleased with what Brett had done so far with South Beach Security.

As Sara and he walked away from the training ring, he noticed Trey's cousin and Sara's new fiancé, Jose Gonzalez, leaning against the doorframe of the building, a broad smile erupting on his face as it settled on Sara.

She hurried to Jose's side and kissed him as he wrapped an arm around her waist.

When Brett approached, he held his hand out and said, "Congratulations on the engagement, Pepe."

"*Gracias.* Congrats to you as well on the promotion to the K-9 division," Jose said as he shook Brett's hand.

"Thanks. I hope I don't disappoint. I know Trey is keen on the K-9s taking off for the agency," Brett said. He owed Trey for believing in him after what had happened in Iraq.

"It was a rocky start what with the serial killer here at the kennels, but I'm sure you and the other agents Sara trains will be up to the challenge," Jose said and playfully squeezed Sara closer.

"I know Brett and Mango will be up for anything," Sara said, no indecision in her voice.

Brett smiled and dipped his head in appreciation for her trust in him and his new K-9 partner's capabilities, which were a testament to her training skills.

As they walked toward the former kennel owner's home where Sara was living with Jose, Brett bid them goodbye and peeled off to head to his car, Mango loping at his side. He buckled the pittie into the front seat and rubbed her head affectionately. The dog responded with a happy lick of his face and a doggy grin.

He was grateful for the dog's love since he knew the pit bull's powerful jaws and muscular body could inflict quite a lot of punishment if necessary. His forearm still ached from the earlier bite, and he was sure he'd have a bruise by the next day even with the padding in the suit. In a real-world situation, extensive thrashing combined with the bite could cause considerable damage.

"You're my girl, Mango," he said and massaged her head

and shoulders again to reinforce the relationship with his partner so that when the time came on assignment, he could trust her to do as commanded.

He just hoped he would have a little more opportunity to train with Mango before that time came. More than anyone, he understood the dangers of not being prepared and what the cost would be, he thought as he rubbed a spot by his collarbone. Beneath his fingers, the ridges of scars were a painful reminder of the price of failure.

But not now. He would be ready when the time came.

THE NIGHT HAD been a killer.

Two of her line chefs had called in sick and a delivery of her porterhouse steaks had gone missing, prompting a last-minute menu change.

Her sous-chef, Melinda, pressed a glass of wine into her hand. "Here, Chef. You need it."

Anita Reyes accepted the glass and peered around her restaurant's kitchen.

All the dinner tickets had been cleared off the rail, and despite being down the two chefs, the others had still been able to clean as they cooked, leaving the kitchen relatively in order.

"Things look pretty good, Chef," she said.

Melinda nodded and gestured toward the back door. "They do, and the butcher promised to get us those porterhouse steaks for tomorrow. Why don't you get some air and enjoy that wine while we finish up."

Anita had been running around all night filling in for the missing line chefs while still doing her own job of making sure that the orders were perfect and ready to go out to diners. Her feet and back ached and sweat dripped down between her shoulder blades from the heat in the kitchen.

A breath of fresh air and sip of a fine wine sounded like heaven.

She pushed through the back door and onto the small landing in the narrow alley between her restaurant and the hotel behind her.

The late-fall night wrapped her in nippy air, making her shiver as it chased away the warmth of the kitchen. The street noises from busy Ocean Drive and Collins Avenue were almost nonexistent in the alley thanks to the buildings sheltering it on either side.

She sat on the stoop, leaned against the brick of the building and sipped the wine, a tasty cabernet franc they'd been lucky to find at a local distributor. The floral vintage pleasantly slipped down her throat, and she breathed a sigh of relief that her killer night was almost over.

Long minutes passed as she relaxed but soon responsibility called her to return to her kitchen and make sure everything was in order so they could start all over again for tomorrow's lunch and dinner crowds. As tired as she was, she reminded herself how lucky she was to have attained her dream of owning her own restaurant, and a successful one at that.

Varadero, her Cubano-Latino fusion restaurant, rarely had an empty seat and dinner reservations were fully booked for the rest of December and into the new year, pulling a smile from her.

But that meant lots of arduous work, and as she slowly rose to return to the kitchen, the door of the hotel across the way burst open as a man flew out and tumbled onto the rough ground in the alley. The man scrambled to his feet, as if ready to run, but a second later a masked man rushed through the door, grabbed him and wrapped an arm around the man's neck.

She recognized the unmasked man as one of the hotel's owners, Manny Ramirez.

Anita froze in place, shocked by the scene playing out before her as the two men grappled in the darkness of the alley.

She had no doubt it was a fight to the death as light suddenly gleamed on a knife blade in the masked man's hand.

He punched the knife into Manny's side and, in a growly voice, said, "You know what we want."

Manny grunted and abruptly bent over from the pain of the knifing. That seemed to break his attacker's hold for a hot second.

A mistake, since Manny was able to take a swipe at his attacker's head. His hand connected and ripped off the mask. Exposed and clearly annoyed, the man tossed Manny away, pulled a gun from beneath his black denim jacket and fired.

A perfect circle marked Manny's forehead as he stood there for a shaky second, surprised by death before he collapsed.

Shock stole Anita's breath, and the sharp sound drew the killer's attention.

He whipped around to stare straight at her, as shocked as she was.

A heartbeat later, he pointed the gun and fired.

She ducked as the bullet whizzed by her head and bit into the brick. A chip flew off and grazed her cheek, propelling her to flee as the warmth of blood trickled down her face.

The man aimed at her again and she tossed her glass of wine at his head.

A perfect strike.

It stunned him long enough for her to dash into her kitchen.

Locking the door behind her, she screamed, "Call 911!"

Chapter Two

The police detective standing across from her seemed better suited for a modeling gig than a cop's life.

Detective Williams was over six feet tall with a lean, muscular physique, ice-blue eyes, boyish dimples and chestnut-colored hair with thick, rumpled waves that fell onto his forehead.

"Do you think you could identify the man who shot at you?" Williams asked, pen poised over a small notepad.

In her mind's eye, the scene she had witnessed barely an hour earlier replayed itself like a movie, pausing at the spot where the mask had come off and then again when the killer had turned his attention to her. She rewound and replayed that section and nodded.

"I'm sure I can."

"Are you sure? I mean, you only saw him for what, a few seconds?" Williams pressed, his gaze narrowed as he scrutinized her.

Her answer was immediate. "Without a doubt. I'll never forget what I just saw."

With a nod, Williams looked toward the two police officers who had been the first ones on the scene in response to her 911 call. He waved a hand in their direction, and when they approached, he said, "Detective Gonzalez has arranged for a sketch artist to work with Ms. Reyes. Please take her to headquarters while I coordinate with the CSI team."

"Yes, sir," said Officer March, a petite young Latina, before turning to her. "If you wouldn't mind following us to our cruiser?"

"Of course," she said, even though the thought of leaving the safe space of her restaurant had her gut clenching with fear.

"I'll lead the way," said Officer Garrett, a strapping Anglo six-footer with shoulders as wide as the doorway and gingery blond hair.

Anita stood and followed the policeman outside, where several other officers kept back a crowd of bystanders who packed the sidewalk and spilled onto the street. It created a traffic backlog of the cars that normally cruised up and down Ocean Drive, wanting to be seen as well as to see what was happening along the popular strip.

There were just so many people, she thought, searching the crowd for the face she had seen in the alley. She had watched one too many crime dramas and knew the suspect often hung back to watch what the police were doing at the crime scene.

For a second, she thought she saw him, and stopped short, heart pounding so hard it felt like it was climbing up her throat.

Officer March immediately came to her side, partially shielding Anita's body with hers. "Do you see something?" she asked.

Peering around again quickly, Anita shook her head. "No, I guess not," she said and continued to the cruiser, where Officer Garrett had opened the door.

She slipped into the back seat, expelling a relieved breath, comforted by the protection of the police cruiser.

But as the car pulled away from the curb, she kept a sharp eye on the crowd, feeling the continued presence of the killer chasing her until they were blocks away and almost at Miami Beach police headquarters on Washington Avenue.

Breathing easier, she settled back into the seat and closed her eyes, but as soon as she did, that night's images flashed through her brain again. The fight. The knife. The perfect little circle in Manny's forehead before he became a lifeless heap on the ground.

She shuddered, wrapped her arms around herself and rocked back and forth, shocked yet again that she'd watched a man die that night.

That she'd almost died.

The cruiser came to a stop in front of the police station, and a second later Officer March slipped from the car to open her door. But as the young Latina stepped onto the sidewalk, a sedan screeched to a halt beside them and the windows on the cruiser's driver side exploded, sending glass flying everywhere.

Officer March hauled Anita down behind the protective barrier of the police cruiser.

"Shots fired. We need backup," she shouted into her radio and returned fire on their attacker.

The sharp retort of the gun had Anita covering her ears and hunkering against the vehicle body for protection.

Officer March cursed beneath her breath. "Officer down. Officer down," she screamed into the radio as, with another angry squeal of tires, their assailant's vehicle peeled away.

Anita shot to her feet in time to watch the late-model Mercedes fishtailing as it sped off.

Officer March raced around to the driver's side of the vehicle, and Anita followed, helping the young officer move her wounded partner to the ground.

"I'm okay," he said with a grimace even though he clearly wasn't. Blood leaked from his shoulder and the many cuts and scratches on his face.

Officer March bent to apply pressure to the wound, but a

mob of other officers and EMTs rushed in to take over. "We've got this," an EMT said as he went to work on Officer Garrett.

"Let's get you inside," Officer March said, and a phalanx of officers surrounded her as they rushed across the plaza in front of the station and into the modern-looking building.

When they burst into the lobby and the officers spread out to take defensive positions at the door, a very pregnant woman walked up to her.

"Ms. Reyes, I'm Detective Gonzalez. Please follow me," she said, but as Anita took a step, her knees suddenly buckled, too weak to support her.

Detective Gonzalez and Officer March were immediately at her side, slipping their arms through hers to offer stability.

"I'm sorry. I feel so stupid," she said.

But Detective Gonzalez reassured her. "It's okay. *You're* okay. We've got you now. It's not every day someone tries to kill you."

No, it wasn't every day someone tried to kill you. Twice.

But she wasn't ready to die.

She drew on every ounce of courage she possessed, straightened her spine and walked with the officers to an interview room.

MIDNIGHT PHONE CALLS were generally not good.

Tonight's call had been no different, Brett thought as Trey and he pulled up in front of the Miami Beach police station.

Crime scene tape surrounded a police cruiser with bullet holes in the doors and shot-out windows. Glass littered the street along with gun shell casings that a CSI team had marked for collection.

A small splotch of blood also stained the pavement and Brett hoped the size of it said the officer had survived the shooting.

Inside the station, they quickly cleared security and went

to meet Trey's wife, Detective Roni Gonzalez. Because of her pregnancy and a bout of bed rest a month earlier, Roni was on desk duty but still working cases.

Roni was waiting for them by her office door along with a cover-model-handsome thirty-something man Brett assumed was her partner.

"Good to see you again, Trey," the man said and shook his boss's hand before turning to him and saying, "Detective Heath Williams."

Brett shook his hand. "SBS K-9 Agent Brett Madison. This is Mango," he said and gestured to the pit bull sitting obediently at his feet.

"Nice to meet you," Williams said as Roni waved them into her office.

"What's up? You need our help?" Trey said and stood by the side of Roni's desk as she sat and rubbed a hand across her baby belly.

"There was a murder tonight in South Beach. We have a witness who the killer tried to take out right in front of the station," Roni said and handed Trey a piece of paper.

"This is the guy?" his boss said, and when Roni nodded, he handed Brett a police sketch of their suspect. A thirty-something man, either Caucasian or Latino, with a strong jaw, sharp, thin nose and small scar beneath one eye. Short-cropped dark hair in a precise fade made Brett think ex-military.

"Pretty bold to try to take someone out right in front of the station," Brett said and handed the sketch back to Roni.

"We feel the same way. That's why we're working on finding the right safe house for our witness, because we think this guy won't stop until she's dead," Williams said and leaned his hands on the top rung of a chair in front of Roni's desk.

"I guess you want to use the penthouse," Trey said, referring to the space that Brett had heard was reserved for the

Gonzalez family when they worked late nights or clients who were either visiting or needed extra security.

Roni nodded. "Just for tonight. If this guy knows I'm on the case and knows the Gonzalez family—"

"Hard not to know them in Miami," Williams said with a shrug of wide shoulders and a touch of facetiousness.

Roni ignored her partner and continued. "He'll probably assume that's what we'll do and might try to go there. We're worried he'll do that while civilians may be present. That's why we're working on finding another safe house. But we can't get that done for another few hours."

"Say no more. Since I figured this was very urgent, Brett and Mango are also here to help protect your witness," Trey said and gestured in their direction.

Mango's ears perked up at the mention of her name and Brett reached down to rub her head. "Mango and I are ready," he said and hoped it didn't sound like he was also trying to convince himself.

"Great. We have an initial witness statement and the sketch. By early morning, we'll be able to move the witness to a safe house. With your help, if that's okay?" Roni said.

Trey nodded. "Whatever you need, SBS is here for you and Miami Beach PD."

"It's appreciated, Trey. This is going to be a high-profile case. Reporters are already leading with this on the local news because the victim is well-known and we had a very public shoot-out in front of the station," Williams said.

Roni lumbered to her feet, her pregnancy belly making her slightly unbalanced, which made Trey slip an arm around her waist.

"You feeling okay?" he asked, clearly still in protective mode considering Roni's issues a month earlier.

"Feeling like a beached whale," she said with a carefree laugh and swept her hand across the large mound of her belly.

With his concerns relieved, Trey motioned for them to head out the door. Once Roni and he were in the lead, Williams, Mango and Brett followed them to an interview room at the far end of the hall.

Roni knocked to announce herself and at the "Come in," they entered.

A shocked gasp filled the air as he stepped inside.

"Brett?" the woman said and as he met her gaze, her surprise transferred to him.

"Anita?" he said and muttered a curse.

Chapter Three

"You two know each other?" Roni asked, her narrowed gaze skipping from Anita to Brett and back to Anita.

Intimately, Anita thought, and heat rose to her face, but her embarrassment was quickly replaced by anger at seeing the man who had ghosted her so many years earlier. A man she'd loved with all her heart.

Body tight with tension, she gestured to Brett and, in what she hoped was a neutral voice, said, "I was a cook at a place not far from where Brett was stationed in North Carolina."

"Anita made the best chicken and rice I've ever tasted," Brett said with a forced smile that was bright against his dark, well-trimmed beard but didn't quite reach up into his chocolate-colored eyes.

"It's on the menu at my restaurant," she said, trying to keep the conversation sounding friendly, although with a quick look at Roni, she thought the other woman had caught on that things were anything but friendly between her and Brett.

"Maybe when this is all over, I can get a plate of it," Brett said, sounding chill as well.

"I'd like that," escaped her before she could bite it back. The last thing she wanted was to spend any more time than was necessary with the marine who had broken her heart.

"Hopefully this will be over quickly," Trey said and clapped Brett on the back.

"I'd like that also," she said, wishing for the same thing.

"We're arranging for a safe house, but in the meantime South Beach Security will help in safeguarding you tonight," Roni explained.

"We're taking you to our offices on Brickell Avenue. We have a secure penthouse there. Brett and his K-9 partner, Mango, will stay with you until you move into the police safe house," Trey said.

Brett and her alone together tonight. Luckily not much was left of the night, since Brett and she had never been able to keep their hands off each other. But she'd learned the painful lesson that passion alone wasn't enough to keep a relationship going.

Hopefully the dog, a thick-bodied, medium-sized tan-and-white pit bull, would play chaperone and provide a buffer to keep them from making a mistake they would regret in the morning.

"If you're ready, Trey and Brett will run you over to the SBS offices," Roni said and gestured to the door.

"Ready as I'll ever be, but before I go, I wanted to know how Officer Garrett is doing," she said, mindful of the officer who had been injured earlier.

Roni smiled in appreciation of her concern. "He'll be fine. Bullet went through his shoulder without doing much damage."

"Good to hear. Please thank him for me."

"I will," Roni said and motioned for her to follow the two men and the dog out of the room. They made their way through the labyrinthian halls of the police station to a more secure back exit to the building.

A big, black unmarked SUV sat at the curb, ready to transport her to SBS's secure space.

She prayed Brett and his boss could keep her safe so she could get back to the restaurant that was her life. She'd toiled and worked too hard to let what had happened tonight keep her from her dream.

Brett helped her into the back seat and then harnessed Mango into the seat next to her, issuing the dog a command. The pittie instantly obeyed and sat, obviously well trained and obedient.

They pulled away from the station and were quickly traveling down Washington toward the causeway that would take them up and over Biscayne Bay to Downtown Miami where SBS apparently had their offices. As they drove, she kept a keen eye on the vehicles in and around them, but so did Trey and Brett.

It was clear both were on the lookout, their gazes constantly darting around to take in everything going on as they pulled onto Brickell Avenue. She caught a glimpse of a plant-filled courtyard decorated with Christmas lights and a nativity scene in anticipation of the upcoming holiday. The courtyard was in front of a large glass-and-stone structure, and they drove into an underground lot for the office building.

After parking, Trey and Brett hesitated, making her wonder until Brett said, "We need to make sure we weren't followed."

Long minutes passed until the two men were seemingly satisfied that it was safe to exit the vehicle.

"Wait for us," Brett said, not that she planned on going anywhere without them.

He and Trey immediately charged into action, exiting the vehicle and removing Mango from the dog's seat. Trey checked the area to make sure it was secure before Brett swung around to her side and opened the door.

He stood by her car door, hand close to the holstered gun at his belt while the other held Mango's leash as the pittie stood tucked tight to Brett's leg, as ready for action as her partner.

She stepped from the car and was straightaway sandwiched between Trey and Brett, who provided protection until they slipped inside the building's stairwell and hurried up the stair-case to the lobby. Brett opened the door and delayed for a moment, making sure the area was clear before they hurried across the lobby and to the security area.

Trey paused to say something to the two guards there, and they did a quick look in her direction and nodded.

As they walked to the elevator bank, she heard the click and static of radios as one of the guards relayed instructions to other security people in the building.

Inside the elevator, Trey used a badge to grant access to the penthouse floor, reached into his guayabera shirt pocket and handed Brett a badge. "This will clear you to enter."

"Thanks," Brett said and slipped the badge into his shirt pocket.

In what seemed like only seconds, they soared to the pent-house, which Anita guessed was about twenty stories up from the vista visible outside the windows that made up two of the walls of the immense open space. The downtown buildings jutting up into the night sky seemed harsh against the delicate palm tree fronds dancing on a night breeze and the shifting, crystalline waters of Biscayne Bay. Bright moonlight kissed the bay, making the water glitter like diamonds in the dark. Here and there, Christmas lights were visible inside offices in the buildings and on the buildings themselves. A few of the of-fices even boasted Christmas trees with gifts beneath. Maybe Secret Santas like they did in her restaurant, she thought.

Inside the penthouse, elegant modern furniture somehow created a comfortable atmosphere, making her almost feel at home, especially as she took in the high-end kitchen at one side of the large area. It had everything a chef would need to make a gourmet meal, not that she would be staying there long enough to cook.

Trey gestured toward the kitchen area and said, "The fridge is fully stocked in case you're hungry. I imagine you didn't

have time to eat tonight. There are clean clothes in the second
bedroom if you want to shower and change into something
more comfortable and get some rest."

"I'd like that," she said and offered him a weak smile in
thanks.

Trey nodded and clapped Brett on the back. "I'll let you
get to work. The guards are on alert down below and as soon
as Roni has the address for the safe house, we'll move Anita
there."

"MANGO AND I will make sure she's safe," Brett said and shot
a quick look in Anita's direction.

She had wrapped her arms around herself tightly, and even
though it had been way too many years since he'd last seen
her, he had no doubt she was barely holding it together. Her
face was pale, the lines as tight as her body, which vibrated
from the tension.

He didn't blame her. Most people rarely witnessed a murder and were almost killed themselves, especially twice in
one night.

Reaching out, he trailed his fingers down her upper arm and
said, "Why don't you take a hot shower. It'll help you relax."

She opened her eyes wide and shook her head. "I'm not
sure how I'll ever relax."

He understood. He'd felt the same way after his first battle
as a soldier. He'd never killed a man, much less almost been
killed. It was something that you never forgot. That settled
in your soul, staying with you no matter how hard you tried
to shake it loose.

As her gaze connected with his, she seemed to also understand and took a step closer, as if seeking solace, but then
abruptly jumped away.

He got it. Being close would bring back too many memories. Remind him of how her body fit naturally to his, like they

were two pieces of a puzzle meant to be together. It would feel like a homecoming, but that was the last thing she probably wanted after the way things had ended between them.

Instead, he said, "It's going to be all right. The police and SBS will keep you safe until we catch this guy."

She bit her lower lip, nodded and flipped her hand in the direction of the far side of the room. "Trey mentioned a second bedroom. Is it that way?"

He shrugged. "I've never been up here, but I'm guessing that's the way," he said and followed her to the far side of the space where three doors were visible. When they reached the second door, he stepped ahead to check the area, not wanting to take any chances, although he trusted that the building had been well secured even in advance of their arrival.

Sure enough, they had nothing to fear, and with that he left Anita to shower and returned to the large open space, Mango tucked against his leg.

He unleashed the pittie, rubbed her head and rewarded her with a treat for her good behavior. Searching through the kitchen cabinets, he located a bowl, filled it with water and set it out. Mango eagerly lapped up a drink.

Since he could also use a pick-me-up, he made a pot of coffee, and thinking that a full belly might help Anita relax, he gathered what he needed from the fridge for a Western omelet and started cooking.

He had just finished flipping the omelet when Anita strolled out in University of Miami sweats that were way too big for her. She'd had to roll up both the sleeves and legs of the sweats. The loose folds of the fabric hid the curves he knew were beneath the fleece, and that was a good thing. He'd loved to explore those curves way too much when they'd been together.

Her hair was damp, making it the color of rich cocoa. The darkness of her hair made her amazing green eyes pop against creamy skin. An angry two-inch-long scrape on one cheek marred her otherwise flawless face.

He was about to skim a finger across that wound, but pulled back, certain that was too intimate a touch. Much like this moment was becoming a painful reminder of other mornings spent with her when they'd been a couple.

To break that too-personal feeling, he busied himself with getting plates and cutlery as she sat at the kitchen island.

"THAT SMELLS GREAT," Anita said, watching Brett putter around the kitchen and return with place settings he set on the counter.

He went back to the stove, grabbed the frying pan and came over to scoop out pieces of the omelet onto the plates. After he did that, he said, "Coffee?"

She shook her head. "I don't think I could sleep if I had coffee," she said and then added with a harsh laugh, "Although I don't even know how I can think about sleep with someone trying to kill me."

He laid a hand on hers and squeezed in reassurance. "We'll keep you safe."

She acknowledged his statement with a quick dip of her head, unable to muster the optimism he possessed. But the aromas from the omelet, sweet pepper and onion mingling with the creamy eggs made her stomach grumble with hunger.

"It looks and smells great. You always made a good omelet," she said and immediately wished she could take the words back because they reminded her of what they had once been to each other.

"Thanks. I had a good teacher," he said, and his words elicited the happy but unwanted memory of her showing him how to flip the eggs restaurant-style. There had been lots of runny eggs on the stove and floor, but also a lot of laughter and love.

When he had gone, she had missed that laughter almost more than the sex, although the sex had been...

Fighting that recollection because it created an ache deep inside her, she asked, "How did you end up in Miami?"

He shrugged those wide, almost impossibly broad and muscular shoulders. "I wasn't up for another tour and got a job at a local police force. I was working there when Trey reached out to me about joining SBS."

Motion from the corner of her eye caught her attention. The pit bull moved away from a water bowl and settled herself close to Brett's feet with what sounded like a happy sigh. "And ended up with a K-9 partner."

Brett smiled, bent and rubbed the dog's head and shoulders, which prompted Mango to roll over and present her belly to him, tongue flopping out of her mouth. Her tail wagged enthusiastically, smacking loudly against the wood floor. He rubbed her belly, laughing at the dog's antics.

"Mango's a good dog. Smart. We've only been paired for about three weeks, but she'd been well trained before that," he said with a final rub and returned to finish the last of his omelet.

She dug into the food as well since the fuller her belly got, the drowsier she was getting despite her earlier comments about sleep eluding her.

Brett, apparently picking up on how she was battling to keep her eyes open, said, "Go get some rest. I'll clean up."

In the old days, they'd had a rule that whoever didn't cook had to clean, but those were the old days and now they were in new and uncharted waters. Still, there was comfort in remembering those old patterns even if they were breaking them and even though she didn't want a repeat of those yesterdays.

"Thanks for cleaning and thank you for the omelet. It hit the spot," she said, rose and was about to head to the bedroom when Brett's cell phone rang.

He answered, listening intently. Nodding, he said, "Got it. I'll bring her down."

Swiping to end the call, he said, "The safe house is ready faster than expected. We're good to go if you are."

"I'm good to go," she said although she wasn't sure she was. Despite how things had ended between them years earlier, there was a sense of security and comfort with him there. Going to the safe house felt like taking a step off a cliff. But if that was what she needed to do to have this whole ugly episode finished so she could get on with her life, she was ready to do it.

But was she ready to deal with Brett's sudden return to her life?

Chapter Four

Brett leashed Mango and led the way from the penthouse to where Trey waited for them in the lobby.

"Miami Beach PD has chosen a safe house in Aventura. Small condo in a complex on Marcos Drive," Trey said and handed Brett a printout with the details of the location.

Brett flipped through the pages, wincing at the photo of the ground-level windows, making it easy for anyone to take a shot into the condo. "Doesn't seem all that secure, and I thought they were worried about civilians?" he said and handed the papers back to Trey.

"Killer doesn't know where we're headed and apparently this was the best choice available on short notice. Aventura police are already guarding the location."

With a reluctant nod and quick glance back at Anita, he said, "I'll feel better once we check it out."

"Agreed. Let's get going," Trey said and pushed off to lead them across the lobby and to the parking garage. At the entrance to the stairs, he paused to make sure the area was safe and did the same once they entered the garage.

The men became human shields to protect Anita, surrounding her until they had her out of harm's way in the SUV with Mango sitting beside her.

Trey was at the wheel, alert for any movement out of the ordinary as they pulled onto Brickell Avenue. He turned in the direction of I-95 for the short fifteen-minute-or-so trip to North Miami Beach and the condo in Aventura. In no time they were moving along the expressway. Traffic was light in the very early morning hours, and like Trey, Brett kept an eye out for a possible attack, but all was calm.

As they exited for North Miami Beach and the hospital, a car quickly raced up behind them on a side street.

"Watch your six," Brett warned Trey, who nodded and confirmed, "Roger that."

Trey pulled to the right and slowed, cautious until the car whipped around them and sped off.

"Just someone in a rush," Brett said and relaxed a little as Trey made the last few turns and finally pulled up in front of the complex for the safe house.

It was a nice-looking building with condos that boasted good-sized patios. Unlucky owners faced the parking lot, but those on the opposite side of the building had gorgeous views of the condo's pool and the waters of Maule Lake, Eastern Shores to the left, Greynolds Park to the right and, in the far distance, Oleta River State Park.

It was those views that worried him since they'd be hard to protect against anyone with a rifle who wanted to shoot into the safe house, although he had noticed heavy metal hurricane shutters in one of the photos Trey had given him earlier.

As they neared the entrance to the building, he noticed the Aventura police car parked in front, but instinct had him reaching out to grasp Trey's arm and say, "Let's wait for them to approach."

Trey nodded and slowly inched up behind the police car but with enough space to maneuver around it in the event of an emergency. *Never let yourself get boxed in*, he remembered from his time in the military.

No activity from the cruiser greeted them when Trey

stopped the car, making Brett's gut tighten with worry. Turning slightly in the seat, he said, "Keep your head down, Anita."

She slinked down in the back seat and Brett said, "I'll go check with them."

He hopped out of the car and walked the few feet to the police car. The window didn't open as he approached, heightening his fear that something was horribly wrong.

He was a foot from the driver's door when he realized both officers were slumped over, clearly injured. Possibly dead.

Backpedaling, he had barely reached the SBS SUV when a shot rang out and pinged loudly against the hood of the vehicle. Exposed, he crouched down, raced to his door and hopped back in as another bullet tore into a wooden column by the front entrance of the condo building.

Trey whipped away from the parking lot and raced back onto the street to escape the shooter, who managed another shot against a side window and then the rear window, but luckily the SUV's bulletproof glass held.

Speed-dialing Roni, Trey said, "We were attacked at the safe house. Two officers are down. Send the EMTs."

Roni muttered a curse. "Sending help immediately. Williams will head there to see what he can find out. Where are you taking Anita?"

Brett jumped in with, "We could go back to the penthouse, but it would expose too many civilians to whoever is desperate enough to do something like this."

"Agreed. I'm taking her to one of our safe houses, only… How did he know where the safe house was?" Trey pressed.

A troubled silence followed until Roni said, "We'll see who had access to that info here and in Aventura."

"*Gracias.* I'll see you later," Trey said and ended the call.

Brett was worried about how the leak had happened, but before he could say anything, Anita spoke up.

"Do you really think someone at the police station leaked the location?"

Trey shrugged as he quickly backtracked to I-95. Once he was on the highway, he said, "This shooter—or whoever hired them if it's not the guy you saw—may have the connections to get that info."

"Where are we going?" Brett asked, concerned that whoever it was might also be able to find the location of this new safe house.

"We have a place in Homestead, not far from the air force base. We'll keep Anita there until we figure out what's going on," Trey said and pushed the vehicle's speed on the highway while also staying vigilant to see if anyone was following them.

Brett did the same, watching for anyone or anything that seemed suspicious. Thinking that whoever had shot at them had done it from a distance and probably would not have had time to get into a car to chase them.

But he didn't like such uncertainty because the two officers had been shot at close range, which meant someone else might have been nearby as well.

"I think there are two shooters. One who attacked the officers and another one who shot at us."

Trey dipped his head from side to side as he considered Brett's question. "I agree. It would explain the injured officers and how someone was also taking potshots at us from a distance."

"Great. Two people trying to kill me," Anita said from the back seat, and Mango must have sensed her distress since the dog did a little whine and laid a paw on Anita's thigh.

"Thank you, Mango," Anita said with the barest hint of a smile.

"Whatever is happening, we will protect you," Trey said and shot a quick look at Brett, who reluctantly nodded.

While he'd signed up to work on any assignment South

Beach Security would give him, he'd never expected that it would involve Anita. They had a history, and that history might make things difficult. It could even open a world of hurt if old emotions rekindled between them.

But he bit his tongue, thinking about what would be necessary to safeguard the house until they could figure out who was after Anita and end the threat.

The drive to the SBS safe house in Homestead was nearly an hour, which gave him way too much time to think about the danger Anita was in and how he and Mango were going to protect her, especially if there were two people working together now.

Those thoughts were still whirling through his head as Trey pulled off the highway and navigated the streets leading to a smallish one-story, coral-colored cinder block home. It was a street with well-kept homes, many of which boasted Christmas lights and decorations for the upcoming holiday. The safe house did as well, making it look just like any other home in the neighborhood.

Once Trey had slipped into the driveway and parked, his boss took a moment to peer all around before he said, "I'll open up and make sure it's clear."

"Mango and I will hang back until you give us the go-ahead," Brett said and went into action, opening the back door and freeing Mango so she could hop onto the concrete pad of the driveway.

Trying to act naturally, he walked Mango along the edge of the drive, letting her relieve herself while he waited for Trey to return. All the time he was on high alert, vigilant for anything that seemed out of the ordinary.

When Trey hurried out a few minutes later, he came to Brett's side and handed him the keys to the house.

"Everything is good inside. You're going to need some groceries and other supplies. While you get Anita settled,

I'm going to make a quick run to the store. They'll be open at seven," Trey said and gestured toward the car, where Anita patiently waited.

"Do you think my guarding her is a good idea?" Brett asked in low tones so only Trey could hear, still worried about the complications of spending time with Anita.

"I understand your concerns, but you obviously know her better than anyone else and that's a good thing. It can't be easy for her and if I'm not reading the signals wrong, you care for her," Trey said, clearly determined that Brett stay on this assignment.

"And that's the issue. Emotion clouds your judgment. We both know where that could lead," Brett replied, worried that feelings could get in the way of his decision-making as they had once with disastrous results.

"I know you still blame yourself, but it wasn't your fault, Brett," Trey said and laid a hand on Brett's shoulder, offering reassurance.

"It was my fault. I dropped my guard—"

"Like any of us would in that situation. I trust your judgment," Trey said and peered back toward Anita. "I think she trusts you, too," he quickly added.

Brett tracked his gaze to where Anita sat, staring out the window at the two of them. "I'm not sure that's true, not that it matters."

"It does matter, but I need to get you those supplies," Trey said and jangled the car keys in his face to signal it was time to get going.

With a reluctant nod, Brett clicked his tongue to command Mango, who had been patiently sitting at his feet, to walk with him to the car. After a quick glance around, satisfied everything was still safe, he helped Anita from the SUV.

"Thanks. It was getting a little warm in there," she said as he led her into the home, locking the door behind them.

Once inside, she stood in the living room and did a quick twirl to peer around the space. "This is home for now?"

"For now. Trey went to get some supplies, but hopefully you'll be able to go home soon," Brett said, understanding her concerns.

"I hope so. I can't be away from the restaurant for that long. I need to call my sous-chef and explain. Give her instructions on what to do. I also need to call my parents so they won't worry," Anita said and pulled her phone from her pocket, but Brett quickly laid a hand on hers to stop her.

"I'm pretty sure the police asked you to shut it off and not use it," Brett said.

Anita nodded. "They did, but I really need to let my people know what's happening."

Brett stroked his hand across hers to calm her, but she jerked her hand away, clearly uncomfortable with his touch. "Wait until Trey comes back. He may have a burner phone you can use. We don't want someone tracking your phone to this location."

ANITA NODDED, understanding the why of it even as she started to pace worriedly across the length of the living room.

Her sous-chef could handle things for a day or two, maybe more, if the two line chefs showed up for work. But if not, they'd have to make arrangements for temps and she'd have to change the daily menus. Order supplies.

Brett's hand at the small of her back stopped the whirlwind of worries that had been circling around her brain.

She faced him, shaking her head in apology. "I'm sorry. I have a lot on my mind."

He offered her a sympathetic smile and said, "I could smell the wood burning from way over there. I understand, but it'll be okay."

"The restaurant is my life, Brett. I've worked so hard and

now…" Emotion tightened her throat hard, making it almost impossible to breathe, much less talk.

"It'll be okay," he repeated and went to stroke a hand down her arm but then yanked it back, clearly remembering how she had shunned his touch earlier.

A bump by her leg had her looking down to where Mango was rubbing her head against Anita's calf, also trying to comfort her.

Their care lightened the weight of worry in her soul. Wiping away tears, she smiled feebly and, in a choked voice, said, "It's going to be just fine."

"It is. How about we get the lay of the land and see the rest of the house?"

She nodded and together they did a slow stroll around the one-story building to learn the layout, locating the primary bedroom with its private bathroom. Two other bedrooms shared a Jack and Jill bathroom. A nice-sized eat-in kitchen was right off the living room in the open-concept space. Glass sliding doors by the kitchen table opened onto a patio and nicely landscaped backyard. A white vinyl fence secured the yard and they stepped out into the early-morning light to scope out the backyard.

In all the rooms and the yard, Brett took his time to let Mango nose around, and at Anita's questioning look, he said, "I want her to be familiar with the scents here."

Although he didn't say it, she got it. *In case someone came here who didn't belong.*

They had just returned to the living room when Mango's head shot up and the dog hurried toward the front door and stood there, vigilant. A low, vibrating growl erupted from her at the sound of a car pulling up.

Brett walked to the window closest to the door and drew aside the curtain to reveal the SBS SUV sitting in the driveway. The driver's door opened, and the rear hatch lifted. Trey went to the back and then walked to the front door, carting several large bags.

Brett commanded Mango to heel and opened the door for Trey, who jerked his head in the direction of the car and said, "There are a few more bags in the back."

Brett and Mango flew into action, heading outside to bring in the rest of the purchases as Trey took his haul into the kitchen.

As Trey unpacked, Anita helped him stow the food in the cabinets and fridge, her mind already racing with what she could cook with the various ingredients. Cooking might help keep her from worrying about all that was happening.

"I see Roni has trained you well," she teased since he'd managed to buy a perfect assortment of fresh foods and staples to complement the pantry items she found as she stored things away.

"Very chauvinist of you. I'm actually the cook in the family," Trey teased back with a boyish grin on his handsome face.

"Then Roni is a lucky woman," Anita said.

Trey smiled and quickly added, "The stuff in the cabinets is fresh. We change it out regularly since we never know when we'll need to use this safe house."

A couple of minutes later, Brett and Mango returned with the rest of the supplies. She laughed as she realized Mango was carrying a bag in her powerful jaws.

"She wanted to help," Brett said with a chuckle and toss of his broad shoulders.

As Brett unpacked, she realized those bags held food for Mango as well as toiletries and clothing.

"I thought you might want to change and guessed at the sizes," Trey said as Brett held up T-shirts and jeans.

"Thank you, but I'm hoping I'll be home and in my own clothes soon," she said. That only earned worried looks on both men's faces.

"I hope so, too," Brett said as he opened the refrigerator to stow the milk and cream Trey had purchased. Of course, just the fact that Trey had laid in enough food for a week warned her that going home soon would be unlikely, which reminded her that she had to call her sous-chef and make arrangements for her restaurant and staff and call her parents to tell them she was okay.

"Brett said you might have a phone I could use to call my people and my parents and let them know what's happening," she said.

"I do. I'll get it for you," he said and left her and Brett alone in the kitchen to finish unpacking.

As they put away the last of the groceries, Brett said, "You'll be back at work before you know it. Don't worry."

She gritted her teeth and nodded. What was the sense of arguing when she knew it wouldn't change a thing about her current situation.

Trey returned to the kitchen and handed her a cheap-looking cell phone. "You can use this."

Taking the phone from him, she hurried from the room to have some privacy for the call.

Chapter Five

Brett watched Anita go, understanding her worries about her business, but he had his own concerns, namely keeping her alive.

"I get the feeling you think this might take some time," Brett said.

Trey nodded and leaned close. "Roni called. No leads on this guy. They're running his police sketch against all the databases, but so far nothing. I have Sophie, Robbie and John Wilson working on it as well."

Trey's tech guru cousins worked miracles for SBS and Wilson, Trey's new brother-in-law, had a supercomputer and programs that had helped the police and SBS on various occasions. If they couldn't make something happen quickly, he didn't know who could.

"That's great. What can I do to help?" he asked.

With a shrug, Trey replied, "Besides keeping Anita safe? Once I leave here, I'm going to find out why someone would want Ramirez dead. You're welcome to help me with that."

"If there's a computer here—"

"There's a laptop on the desk in the second bedroom. You can access our network with your own credentials. If you find anything—"

"I'll keep you posted," Brett said just as Anita returned to the kitchen.

"What do we do now?" she asked.

"Brett and I, as well as the rest of the SBS team, are working on identifying the suspect you saw. For now, just get some rest and stay alert," Trey said and hastily added, "I should go back to the office to oversee things."

"I'm not sure I could sleep, but I'll try," she said.

"Take the first bedroom with the bathroom. I need to use the computer in the second room," Brett said with a flip of his hand in the direction of the far side of the house.

Anita nodded, snatched up the clothing that Trey had bought and hurried from the room again. At the sound of the bedroom door closing, Brett said, "She's barely holding it together."

Trey nodded. "Understandable, but luckily she has you. You know her and what she'll need to face this."

Face this? Brett thought. Even he felt the weight of the uncertainty, but he would help her in any way he could.

"I'll take care of her."

Trey nodded and bro-hugged him. "As soon as we have anything, you'll be the first to know."

Brett dipped his head in acknowledgment and said, "I'll start searching for any dirt on Manny Ramirez."

With that, he walked Trey to the front door. Once his friend had left, Brett locked the door and returned to the kitchen to feed Mango before he started researching the hotel owner.

The pit bull greedily gobbled down the kibble, making Brett laugh.

He bent and rubbed the dog's sides after she finished and teased, "How you don't choke is beyond me."

The dog answered him with an almost knowing grin and a kibble-scented lick of his face.

"Let's get to work," he said and issued a hand command for the dog to follow him to the second bedroom, where, as promised, a laptop sat on a small desk.

He tried to make himself comfortable on the wooden chair,

but his holster kept on banging on the furniture's side, forcing him to remove it and place it on the desktop. Powering up the laptop, he started with simple searches on the internet to get a sense of who Manny Ramirez had been.

Luckily, a local magazine had done a piece on Ramirez as part of a Latino Heritage Month celebration. The article was a glowing tribute to how Ramirez had escaped Cuba as a young boy during the Mariel boatlift in 1980 and earned scholarships to a local university known for its hospitality management program. After graduating with honors, Ramirez had launched his career by laboring in low-level positions until he'd worked his way up to management roles in a variety of boutique hotels. He'd used those as a launching pad for jobs with a large luxury chain until somehow finally purchasing a run-down South Beach hotel with a business partner. Together, the men had turned the location around and made it one of the most well-known properties in the area.

It seemed like a success story on its face, but something niggled Brett's consciousness. Mainly, how the two men had managed to find the money to buy the building, which even in its shabby state had to have been worth a great deal of money.

Searching the web, he found a website that listed similar properties for sale and whistled as he discovered a hotel in the area that was on the market for well over twenty million dollars. A lot of money for two men who hadn't owned any property before that.

Unless, of course, they had partners who had bankrolled the purchase, he thought, mulling over that possibility and who might be involved.

That had him returning to his research until Mango raised her head from where she had been sitting at his feet.

"What is it, Mango?" he asked, then rose and grabbed his holster, slipping it back on his belt.

Mango immediately raced toward the door of the primary

bedroom, where she pawed at the bottom of the door, clearly sensing that something was wrong.

Hand on his gun, Brett listened at the door. A strangled cry rent the air, worrying him. He knocked on the door. "Everything okay in there?"

ANITA WIPED AWAY the last tears of the crying jag she'd allowed herself. Straightening from the bedspread, she hurried to the door, all the while hoping Brett wouldn't take note of the tears.

He hated tears. Hated to see women cry. He'd let that slip once when they'd been lying together after making love. Not long before he was supposed to ship out to Iraq, which had been the reason for her tears that night.

Sucking in a deep breath, she forced a smile and opened the door.

Brett's gaze swept over her features, apparently seeing too much since he reached out and drew her into his arms, offering solace.

She didn't fight him this time since the warmth and feel of his body supplied a sense of security and homecoming she'd been lacking for way too long.

The long hours at the restaurant had left her little room for a personal life, and the few times she'd tried, the relationships just hadn't felt right.

Right, like what she was feeling at that moment, held in his powerful arms. No matter how it had ended between them, Brett had always been the one man who had made her feel like she'd found home.

"I'm okay," she finally mumbled into his broad chest when prompted by Mango butting her head against her leg.

She absentmindedly reached down to pet the pit bull, but then yanked her hand back, remembering that Mango was a service animal.

"I know I'm not supposed to treat her like a pet, only she's just so friendly," she said.

Brett inched away slightly and peered down at Mango. "She isn't a pet, but she's taken a liking to you, and she is here to protect you. Right, girl?" he said and bent to affectionately rub the dog's ears.

What looked like a grin spread across Mango's mouth and she bumped her head against Brett's leg, as if confirming what he'd said.

"She's really special," Anita said, tempted again to pet the animal, and at Brett's nod, she did, earning a doggy kiss on her hand.

"She is. Like I told you, I haven't had her long, but she's smart and fearless. When I took her through the obstacle course, she didn't hesitate to do things like the tunnel, which freaks out a lot of dogs."

"I'm glad to hear you're happy with her," she said, especially since she supposed Brett and Mango intended to work together for several years.

"I am," he said and wavered, focusing on her face intently. "Are you sure you're okay?"

Her smile came freely this time and she nodded. "I am. What were you doing?"

"Research into Manny Ramirez to figure out why someone would want to take him out," he said and rose to his six-feet-plus height, reminding her once again of his physical power and presence.

Why someone would want to kill Manny had been on her brain for hours. With a shrug, she said, "He seemed like a nice guy. He was very welcoming and helpful when I first opened the restaurant."

"What about his partner?" Brett asked.

Anita gestured toward the kitchen. "Why don't I make us some tea while we discuss him."

She always found tea calming, unlike coffee, which made her hyper.

Brett nodded and flipped his hand in the direction of the second bedroom. "Let me grab my laptop in case we want to look up something."

"Great," she said and hurried to the kitchen, where she located a kettle and a tea box filled with an assortment of brews.

She filled the kettle and set it on the heat, pulled mugs from the cabinets and laid them out on the table.

When her stomach did a little growl, she remembered that Trey had bought cookies, possibly because he knew his friend Brett had a wicked sweet tooth. Going to another cabinet, she found the package and placed several cookies on a plate she set in the center of the round table in the eat-in section of the kitchen.

The house was actually a great starter home with a kitchen that had her itching to cook. Then again, most kitchens had her itching to cook, and since it seemed they'd be there at least for the night, she intended to make dinner later.

Brett entered the room, placed his laptop on the kitchen table and flipped the lid open on the tea box. "Earl Grey for you, right?"

She nodded and smiled, comforted that he had remembered her favorite. In turn, she pulled out two black tea bags and handed them to him. "I know you think tea is dirty brown water—"

"And I like it as dark as I can get it," he said, then accepted the tea bags and placed them in the mug.

"I could make you coffee if you'd like," she said, but he waved her off.

"Dirty brown water is fine. I know tea calms you," he said with a chuckle.

She sat next to him to wait for the kettle to whistle and said, "You were investigating Ramirez?"

He nodded, swung the laptop around and powered it up again. "I am. We're trying to figure out why someone would want him dead. Did you know him at all?"

Anita tried to recall what she remembered about the man. "He and his partner bought the hotel about six months before I signed the lease for the restaurant. I understand most people in the area were happy about it because it would mean more tourists and possibly more business."

Brett nodded and asked, "Do you know how he got the money to buy it?"

Anita delayed, feeling awful about speaking ill of a dead man. But then again, wouldn't it be worse to let his death go unavenged? With a shrug and bobble of her head, she said, "Rumors said it was more than just Ramirez and his partner in the business."

"Meaning?" Brett asked as he typed something into the laptop, possibly his password.

"I heard from another hotel owner that there was dirty money behind the purchase."

Brett digested what she'd said. "Could be just bad blood because that owner was afraid of losing business to a new place."

She nodded. "Could be, but I heard it from more than one person who didn't have an ax to grind."

"And where there's smoke, there's fire," Brett said and typed something else into the computer.

"What are you doing?" she asked, leaning over to read what was popping up on the screen.

"Checking the property records to see if any mortgages are listed. If they are, that might dispel any rumors about the dirty money," he said and turned the laptop slightly so she could see the results more clearly.

"There's a mortgage listed. They got a loan from a bank," she said, but shook her head. "What about all the renovations? That loan barely covered the cost of the hotel."

"Are you sure?"

With a certain bop of her head, she said, "I remember the listing price because I saw it when I was searching for a restaurant space I could lease. Unless they got a huge deal, that mortgage was only for part of the purchase and none of the renovations."

"That confirms some of the info I found before. I'll send this to Roni and Trey and see what they can do with it," he said and tapped away on the computer to email his colleagues.

The whistle of the teakettle made her pop up, grab a pot holder and shut off the stove. She picked up the kettle and poured the hot water into the mugs with their tea bags.

While Brett wrote his email, she grabbed some cream and sweeteners for herself, since he took his dirty brown water as black as he could, and prepped her tea.

"What else do you know about Ramirez and his partner? Anyone they work with?" Brett asked.

Cradling the mug in her hands, Anita found the warmth was comforting, as was the citrusy fragrance of the bergamot. She dipped her head from side to side as she considered everything she'd heard about the hotel or the two men who owned it. There had been the rumors about the purchase, of course, but not much else, except...

"I think Ramirez liked to bet on the horses and sports games."

Chapter Six

"Gambling? Did he do a lot of it?" Brett asked, imagining the kind of trouble Ramirez could have gotten into if his luck hadn't been good.

She nodded. "He invited me to go with him to some big racing event. At Waterside Park, I think. He said he had friends with connections and a VIP suite."

Brett hopped online and went to the website for the racetrack. A number of events were listed, and he read them off to her. "International Derby. Hibiscus Invitational Meet. Paloma Challenge—"

She jabbed her index finger in his direction to stop him. "That's the one. The Paloma Challenge. It's some fancy racing, music and food event. Ramirez even hinted that if I went, he would make the connections for me to be one of the featured chefs for next year."

"Makes me wonder how much one of those VIP suites might cost," he said and whistled after a quick search on the internet revealed the price. "Luxury suites can run over fifty thousand plus catering and liquor."

"Ouch. His connections obviously had big bucks."

"Possibly dirty big bucks, you said, right? I'll send that info, too, and see if they can get the names of who rented those VIP suites," Brett said and drafted another email to Roni and Trey so they could do additional research.

He got an email back almost instantly.

Video meeting tonight. Twenty hundred.

Confirming he'd be available, he let Anita know about the meeting.

"I hope they've made some progress," she said, shoulders drooping.

"I know you're worried about the restaurant, but we need to keep you safe," he said and stroked a hand across her shoulders, offering comfort.

Her lips thinned into a tight slash, and she nodded. "I know. I'm just not used to being away and cooped up like this."

He remembered how she had been quite active, often jogging or hiking when she wasn't working at the restaurant where he had first met her.

Deciding that he'd already made some headway in their investigations and that he had to keep Anita sane for the moment, he jerked a thumb toward the rear of the house. "Mango could use some exercise. A walk isn't a good idea, but there is that backyard out there. We could let her have some fun."

Anita peered at the pit bull, who gazed up at her adoringly. "I'd like that."

He shut down the laptop, rose and grabbed some treats from a bag that Trey had bought.

"*Kemne*, Mango," he said and reinforced the command with a hand signal, moving his palm toward himself.

Mango immediately hopped to her feet and followed the two of them out the sliding glass doors to the small square of fenced-in yard behind the home. There were well-tended flowers planted around the edges, adding bright spots of color against the white vinyl fence and emerald of the tropical plants in the beds. By the back door was a mesh bag with an assortment of sports balls, and Brett took out a tennis ball.

He tossed it toward the back of the yard and before he could even utter the command, Mango was chasing after the ball and returning to drop it at his feet. "Good girl," he said and rubbed the dog's ears.

He offered the ball to Anita, who tossed it and laughed as Mango shot off to retrieve the object and eagerly bring it back to her. She bent to rub Mango's head and chuckled as the dog hopped up to lick her face.

"*Lehni*, Mango. *Lehni*," he said and pointed to the ground to reinforce his down command.

Mango swiftly obeyed, but Brett could swear the dog seemed unhappy that he'd instructed her away from Anita. To reward her for obeying, he fed her a treat and rubbed her head. "Good girl. I know you love Anita, but you have to listen to me."

Grabbing the ball, he tossed it again and they continued playing the game with him and Anita alternating the throws. It seemed to do Anita well to escape her thoughts about what was happening. Her face lost some of its paleness and a healthy pink glow spread across her cheeks. Her smile was bright and reached up into her green eyes, making them sparkle like a finely cut emerald.

She could distract him from what he had to do, and more than once he had to force himself to keep his mind on the area around them, vigilant for any signs of danger. Luckily the hour passed pleasantly with them playing with Mango and him reinforcing some of the commands they'd been working on together at the new SBS K-9 training facilities.

More importantly, the hour passed without a threat, and he hoped that would continue.

"We should probably head back in," he said, keen eyes surveying the area around the backyard to make sure everything was secure.

At the door to the kitchen, he held out his arm to block Anita's entry, and at her questioning gaze, he said, "Just want to make sure it's safe."

Especially after what had happened just hours earlier at their supposedly secure safe house.

He opened the door and, with a hand command, confirmed the "go check" instruction with "*Revir*, Mango. *Revir*."

Mango raced into the house. The patter of her nails on the floor sounded loudly as she did a loop around the primary areas of the home. Quiet told him she had hit the bedrooms, which were carpeted, before the sound of her approaching again on the hard wooden floors indicated that it was safe inside.

The pit bull sat just inside the door, head tilted slightly as if to say, "Why aren't you coming in?"

"Good girl, Mango." He rubbed the dog's head and fed her a treat as Anita and he entered the house.

"I didn't realize you could train a dog to search a home like that," Anita said while walking toward the fridge.

"It takes some training, but it's useful. Psychiatric service dogs are trained to do that so they can reassure patients who are fearful of people being in their space," he said and leaned on the counter beside her as she started taking things out of the fridge.

At his questioning glance, she said, "I figured I'd start prepping some things for dinner. Cooking relaxes me."

He nodded and flipped a hand in the direction of the computer. "I'll get to work while you cook." He wanted to say that it would relax him to know they were making some progress on the case, but he bit it back, knowing it would kill the happy mood she was in.

With that in mind, he sat at the kitchen table, opened his laptop and logged in to the SBS network to continue his research.

THERE WAS SOMETHING calming about the way the knife cut through the carrots. The sharpness of the blade easily broke the flesh, creating nice sticks she chopped into smaller pieces for the stew she'd decided to make. Stew was comfort food and boy did she need comfort, although having Brett nearby, as complicated as that was, helped, as did Mango's presence.

She'd heard stories about the kind of damage that pit bulls could do. Luckily Mango seemed to like her, she thought with a quick look at the dog, who had settled herself at Brett's feet as he worked.

Armed with that sense of safety, Anita tossed the carrots into the pot, where she already had onions, celery and beef cooking in the fat from the bacon she had rendered to start the meal. Bacon always added welcome smokiness and salt.

She stirred the mixture, careful to cook it slowly, building a nice caramelization of the beef and vegetables in the pot. The brown bits would add a ton of flavor to the sauce for the stew.

When she was satisfied the mixture was ready, she deglazed the pot with some red wine, also courtesy of Trey's shopping. Roni was a lucky woman if Trey was this conscientious at home.

Scraping the bottom and sides of the pan, she got all the brown bits off, added stock and then her grandmother's mix of spices for her *carne con papas* stew. Oregano, pepper and bay leaves would add more flavor to the sauce. She'd add the potatoes later.

"Smells great," Brett said from beside her, startling her and making her jump. She had been so focused she hadn't heard him approach.

"Just me," he said, then laid a hand on her shoulder and gently squeezed to calm her.

Heart pounding, she splayed her hand over her chest and said, "A little jumpy."

"Understandable," he said, so close, the warmth of his breath spilled across her forehead. The smell of him, so familiar, both restored calm and unsettled her.

It was difficult to have him so close. The hard feel of his

arm next to hers. And his hand, so strong and possibly deadly, yet incredibly gentle as well.

It roused memories of the way it had once been between them, and as she looked up and met his gaze, it was clear he was thinking much the same thing.

She gestured with an index finger, pointing between the two of them. "This doesn't make any sense considering how things ended."

His lips tightened into a line as sharp as her knife. "I never meant for it to end that way."

She raised an eyebrow in both question and challenge. "With you ghosting me?"

Looking away, he abruptly shook his head and released a long, rough exhale peppered with an awkward rush of words. "I didn't mean to, only…the deployment wasn't going well and…you had mentioned a new job in another town. I didn't want to do anything that might hold you back."

It took a long moment for her to take in all that he'd said, but then she blurted out, "I'm sorry the deployment didn't go well for you but maybe talking to someone about it might have helped."

And she'd taken the new job mainly to get away from Brett and any memories of him.

BRETT WASN'T SURE that anything at that time could have helped him deal with what he'd experienced on the battlefield and the lingering effects of it.

"Maybe. It's not the kind of thing you share, especially with…civilians," he reluctantly admitted and quickly tacked on, "I wanted to look for you when I got back, but I couldn't. I wasn't the same man and wouldn't have been good for you. But I'm sorry I hurt you. I never meant to do that."

"And here we are now. What do they say? Fate works in mysterious ways?" she said with a shrug, then turned her attention back to dinner and covered the pot to let the stew simmer.

"It does, only…this isn't quite how I pictured a reunion and…"

His long hesitation had her glancing back up at him. "We can't trust anything we're feeling?"

He nodded. "You can say that. We've got a past and now this unpredictable present."

"But definitely not a future?" she pressed, narrowing her gaze to try to read what he was thinking.

The last thing Brett wanted to do was to hurt her, but developing feelings for her again could make him hesitate when he had to act or take unacceptable risks. That had cost him once dearly. It was the reason he wasn't the same happy-go-lucky guy she'd once loved. For those reasons, he gave a final squeeze to her shoulder and whispered, "I'm not sure this is the best time to think about a reunion."

The muscles in her jaw clenched and her lips flattened into a slash of displeasure. Her eyes, those gorgeous emerald-colored eyes, lost any luster and grew cold and distant.

"You're right. It isn't," she said and pointed toward the kitchen table, where his laptop and papers sat, waiting for him.

"I'm going to get back to work." He didn't wait for her reply before returning to the table and settling in to do more research on Manny Ramirez, his partner and any of the people he associated with at the races or his hotel.

In more than one photo he noticed the same few faces. He saved those photos to a file on his laptop and made a list of their names.

One name popped out at him: Anthony Delgado.

Brett hadn't been directly involved with the SBS case involving a possible serial killer at the location of the new SBS K-9 training center. He'd been working on another assignment, but he'd heard Delgado's name mentioned in connection with the kennel investigation.

He had no doubt Trey would immediately zero in on that name as well since it was way too much coincidence that a real estate developer with shady connections would also be tied to Ramirez.

Occam's razor. The simplest explanation is often the most likely answer.

Except that seemed a little too simple and obvious and stupid.

Why would Delgado do something to draw attention to himself?

Setting aside Delgado, Matt researched the other names on the list. Many of them were connected to horse racing and another name caught his attention: Tony Hollywood.

The mobster's name had been tossed around during another investigation a few months ago involving sabotage at a local racehorse stable.

SBS K-9 Agent Matt Perez was now engaged to the owner of the stable. He made a note in the file to have someone at SBS chat with Matt and his fiancée, Teresa Rodriguez, about the names on his list.

As he worked, the sound of Anita toiling in the kitchen and the smell of dinner accompanied him, creating a very homey and comforting environment. For a moment he could almost forget that they were dealing with a life-and-death situation... until he reminded himself that it was Anita's life at stake.

Anita, who I still care about more than I should.

He glanced in her direction. She was busy stirring something on the stove, slight frown lines across her forehead as she focused.

She had slipped into the cotton shorts and T-shirt that Trey had bought for her. They were slightly large but did nothing to hide her generous Cuban curves. Curves he was well familiar with and created an unwanted reaction that had him shifting uncomfortably in the chair.

He muttered a curse beneath his breath, but it had apparently been loud enough to draw her attention.

She stopped stirring and glanced in his direction. "Did you find something interesting?"

Chapter Seven

Yes, you.

He bit it back and instead said, "I'm wondering what you're so busy stirring."

The barest hint of a smile slipped across her face. "I remembered you liked cheesy polenta and thought that might be fun with the stew instead of rice."

"Totally fun," he said while reminding himself that nothing about what was happening was fun. But faking it made it easier to deal, especially for Anita.

Because of that, he shot to his feet and said, "I'll set the table so we can eat before the meeting."

The meeting.

Anita had gotten so involved with prepping dinner that she'd almost forgotten about the meeting. And about Brett. *Almost* being the operative word.

It was impossible to forget that the man she'd loved with all her heart was now just feet away. When he'd stopped writing or video calling her so many years earlier, she'd feared that he'd been killed, but after asking around, she'd learned that he was alive and well. Physically well anyway.

She'd gotten the sense from his earlier awkward response that the aftereffects of his deployment still possibly lingered. She told herself not to care. Not to wonder how he liked being in Miami and working with his old friend Trey Gonzalez.

She forced herself to do what she did best, ladling spoonfuls of the polenta into large bowls and topping it with the beef stew, hoping it would soothe their nerves. To finish the dish, she sprinkled fragrant chopped parsley for a bit of freshness and frizzled onions she'd fried for texture.

She picked up the bowls and took them over to the table. After, she returned to the kitchen, grabbed the bottle of wine she had opened to cook and went to pour some for Brett.

He waved her away and said, "No, thanks. I need to stay clear."

She did a small pour for herself, more to savor it with the meal she'd prepared than to calm herself. She didn't think there was much that would help ease both her fear and the conflicting emotions about Brett.

Returning the wine bottle to the kitchen counter, she poured water for Brett and brought it to the table, where he was waiting for her to eat.

"Go ahead, please. Don't let it get cold," she said as she sat, but he held off until she was in her chair to fork up some of the polenta and stew.

As soon as it was in his mouth, he hummed in appreciation and said, "This is delicious. Thank you."

"You're welcome. I figured we needed some comfort food with all that's happening."

Brett nodded and forked up another big helping that he ate before he said, "I'm sorry this is happening, but we'll get you home as soon as we can."

"That would be great. I worry about being away from the restaurant," she confessed.

He hesitated for a second, ate another healthy portion and then said, "You always wanted your own place. When did you open it?"

"About three years ago. I started with a food truck and that did well. At one of the food and wine festivals in South Beach

I made some connections that landed me on a few television cooking competitions. I was lucky enough to win," she said, then picked up her glass and took a sip of the wine.

"It wasn't just luck. You worked hard and you're a great chef," he said and fixed his gaze on her, as if he wanted her to see the sincerity in his words.

She smiled, appreciating his support. "Thank you. The competitions let me build a nest egg to open the restaurant, and once I did I got some nice reviews and more television appearances. It was demanding but worth it."

"Wow, I'm with a celebrity chef," he said, a note of playful awe in his voice.

Laughing and shaking her head, she said, "Not much of a celebrity but it is fun to be on television."

DEFINITELY MORE FUN than the way she might be plastered all over television now because of the murder, he thought, but didn't say, wanting to keep the discussion upbeat and casual. She'd had enough of death and destruction for the moment and would have more of it once they had their meeting later.

"I've never been on television. What's it like?" he asked and ate as she described the chaotic atmosphere of the televised cooking competitions, the pressure to win as well as the hectic moments as they filmed the segments.

He finished his bowl well before she did, rose and got himself another helping because the food was too delicious not to have seconds. But seeing she still had way too much on her plate because she'd been telling him about her television appearances, he said, "I'm sorry. I didn't mean to keep you from eating."

"It's not that. I'm a mindful eater. I guess it's a downside of being a chef. I'm always analyzing everything I eat. The mouth feel. If it's lush. The textures and taste," she said and finally scooped up a larger forkful.

He got it. He was always on the lookout for things that were out of place or could be dangerous to whomever he was protecting, he thought but didn't say.

Keep it casual, he reminded himself.

"You always could pick out all kinds of different flavors and textures when we went out for dinner," he said and winced, hoping his words wouldn't rouse unhappy memories.

A wistful smile drifted across her face. "We used to have fun…" she began, then shook her head and quickly switched gears. "How did you end up in Miami?"

With a shrug, he said, "It's a long story."

She wiggled her fingers in front of her in a come-and-share way. "I think we have all night at least."

He laughed harshly since he couldn't disagree with that. "I met Trey when we were Stateside, and I was working as an MP. When I deployed, I ended up working alongside him during our tour."

"You were both in Iraq at the same time?" Anita asked to confirm and resumed eating.

Brett nodded. "We were. It was hot, dusty and dangerous but we survived. When we came back, Trey headed home to Miami, and I stayed near the base. Found a job as a K-9 officer with a small local police force and did college part-time until I got my degree."

"I guess you didn't like being a cop?" she said, picking up his vibes.

With a dip of his head, he said, "It's much harder now, but I loved the job. Loved helping people. I just missed being near a big city. Small-town life wasn't for me."

"Why not go back to your family on Long Island?" she asked as she finally finished her bowl of polenta and stew.

He shrugged and said, "I was thinking about doing that when Trey reached out to me. He'd taken over the reins at SBS and was starting a new division. He remembered my work with the K-9s and wondered if I would be interested in working with him."

"And the rest is history," she said with a laugh and shake of her head.

"The rest is history," he repeated and chuckled.

"And here we are," she said and held her hands palms up, as if to say, "What now?"

He wished he knew what would come next for them, but for now his sole focus had to be on keeping Anita safe. He couldn't allow any distractions that would keep him from that, including Anita.

"I'll help you clean up so I can get ready for the meeting," he said and jumped up.

"You mean so *we* can get ready for the meeting. I don't plan on just waiting around while someone tries to kill me."

She also stood, picked up their bowls and took them to the kitchen sink.

Admiring her determination, he said, "*We* will get ready."

He joined her at the sink and together they rinsed and loaded the dishes into the dishwasher, the actions a familiar pattern since they had done it so many times when they had been dating. As it always had, it calmed and brought a sense of peace he'd often lacked while serving in the Marines.

It was with that peace that they sat together at the table for the video meeting with his colleagues at SBS.

When the image snapped to life on his laptop screen, he transferred it to a nearby television, so they'd have a larger image. Trey, Mia, Roni, Robbie and Sophie sat at the conference room table in the SBS offices.

"Good evening," Trey said, beginning the meeting.

"Is it a good evening?" Brett said, hoping his boss and friend might have good news.

The grim look on Trey's face immediately provided the answer. "Unfortunately, we're not any closer to finding out how the safe house was compromised. Because of that, we're going to be keeping Anita at our location for the time being."

Brett nodded. "Understood."

"Good," Trey said and pushed on with the meeting. "We looked at the info you sent over. We uncovered much of the same information. Delgado came to our attention during the kennel investigations."

Brett knew there was possibly more and said, "What about Hollywood?"

Trey nodded. "When we helped Teresa Rodriguez with the attacks at her stable, we also learned about Tony Hollywood. He's a mobster the FBI believes is involved in some illegal activities at the racetrack. I put my money—no pun intended—on Hollywood having a connection to this murder given Ramirez's possible gambling."

"I think we should focus on Hollywood," Brett said and everyone at the SBS table nodded in agreement.

"Good. Because of that, we've reached out to the FBI agents who were investigating Hollywood to see if they can add anything to the mix," Trey said.

"We also have John running Hollywood through his program to see if it confirms our suspicions," Mia said, referring to her newlywed husband and the software he had created that could predict the possibilities of almost anything.

At Anita's questioning look, Brett leaned close and whispered, "I'll explain later."

With a quick bob of her head, the meeting continued with Roni joining in. "The FBI believes Hollywood runs some kind of gambling ring. Fixing races, loan-sharking, illegal betting. It's possible Ramirez was involved or owed Hollywood money and our suspect was sent to clean things up."

"I'm sorry to say this, Roni, but it seems possible that if a police officer owed someone money, they could be pressured to supply information to Hollywood or his associates. Like the safe house location," Brett said.

Roni's face hardened and she frowned at his suggestion, but with the slightest nod, she reluctantly said, "It's possible. My partner, Detective Williams, is investigating that angle."

"Thank you, Detective. I know that can't be easy," Anita said, clearly reading the other woman's upset.

"It isn't, but we'll check every possible angle to make sure you're safe, Anita. Believe that," Roni said, then winced and rubbed a hand across her baby belly. "Sorry, the baby kicked. Sometimes I wonder if she wants to come out early and in time for Christmas," she said with a laugh.

Christmas, Brett thought. It was barely three weeks away, but the holiday was the last thing on his mind.

"Hopefully we'll all be home for Christmas," Anita said and shot Brett an encouraging glance.

"Hopefully," he echoed and wondered if he might some-how be spending Christmas with her as he often had in the past. He'd even taken her home to Long Island one Christmas, making his family wonder if she was "the one."

And she had been until everything that had happened in Iraq, he thought, and shook those thoughts from his head to focus on the meeting.

"In the meantime, Robbie and I are searching various sources for more information on Hollywood and his associates. We're also using facial recognition software to see if we get any hits against the artist's sketch of our suspect," Sophie said.

Robbie seconded that with, "We'll find something. I'm sure of it."

Brett didn't doubt that. Trey's tech guru cousins and fellow SBS agents were NSA-level smart. Together with Mia's tech genius husband, he was sure they'd find out more before the FBI or police would. They were just that good.

"I don't doubt it. I'll keep working at my end as well," he

said, hoping he could also help to bring this investigation to a quick close.

Once that happened…

He didn't want to think about what that would mean for him and Anita now that they'd been thrown together again.

"Great," Trey said and clapped his hands as if to signal that they were done. His next words confirmed it. "Let's all get to work on these various leads, but also get some rest. We need to be sharp if we're going to break this case and get Anita home safe and sound for the holidays."

After everyone echoed his sentiments, Trey ended the video call, leaving Brett and Anita at the table, peering at each other.

"Are you okay with all that?" he asked, wondering what she might be thinking about their actions and how they impacted her life.

ANITA SUPPOSED SHE'D have to be okay with all that they were doing to keep her safe.

"What choice do I have? You said you'd explain about Mia's husband," she said, puzzlement on her face as she recalled Mia's mention of him during the meeting.

Brett nodded. "She married John Wilson, the tech billionaire, a couple of months ago."

"And he has some kind of magic program?" she asked, still confused by the connection to the well-known and eccentric billionaire.

"You could call it that. His program sucks in data from all over and analyzes it to predict the actions that might occur, the likelihood that suspects are involved in a crime. Even victims before they become victims. All kinds of things like that," Brett explained.

It seemed a little woo-woo to her, and while she wasn't a Luddite, she preferred things she could touch and feel, which was likely why she was a chef. She loved the hands-on aspect of cooking. It grounded her.

"It sounds almost sci-fi to me, but if it works…"

"It works. I've seen it in action, but it's still hard to believe although AI can do a lot of amazing—"

"And scary things," Anita jumped in. She'd seen deep fakes and other worrisome AI-generated elements.

Brett nodded. "Definitely scary so it's good Wilson is on our side. He lets SBS use his supercomputers for a lot of our work and that gives us a huge advantage over the authorities."

"I'm glad also. I'd love for this nightmare to be over quickly," she said and gestured toward the bedrooms. "I'm going to watch some television in my room. I don't want to bother you when you work."

"You can watch out here. When I'm concentrating, nothing bothers me," he said and jerked his head in the direction of the large TV mounted on the wall and the very comfy-looking couch with its soft, deep cushions.

She tracked his gaze to the couch and large TV. "Thanks, I will."

It wasn't because of Brett that she'd stay there, she told herself. No, it wasn't, she argued internally but at the same time she couldn't deny that having him nearby brought a maelstrom of emotions. Peace, comfort and that something else she didn't want to acknowledge yet. She was still working through the hurt caused by his ghosting her and reminding herself that she had her own life now. One she'd fought hard to achieve, and which didn't have time for any kind of relationship. Especially one as complicated as it would be with Brett.

Even with all those misgivings, she snuggled into the welcoming couch cushions and flipped on the television, surfing through the channels until she found one of those treacly sweet movies that drew her into the forgetfulness of happily-ever-afters. This one was about two chefs, their nieces and an unexpected cooking competition.

Perfect, she thought as she gave herself over to the entertainment and grew drowsy.

As her eyes drifted closed, the actors on the screen melded into her and Brett, bringing visions of a happy, carefree life. But as she closed her eyes, a sudden abrupt movement roused her.

Chapter Eight

Brett had been deep into the info on the screen when Mango's head shot up.

The pit bull stood and stared toward the sliding doors that led into the backyard and growled.

A shadow shifted across the darkness.

Brett shot to his feet as one of the glass doors shattered, sending shards flying into the room.

"Get down, Anita," he shouted and whipped out his gun, but before he could shoot, Mango launched herself at the intruder and clamped down on the man's arm.

He dropped his gun and it clattered onto the floor.

Brett issued the attack command to reaffirm Mango's actions. "*Útok*, Mango. *Útok*."

The man was screaming and beating on Mango's head with his free hand.

Brett took a step in the intruder's direction but suddenly a second man burst through the broken door, forcing him to confront the new attacker.

"Hold or I'll shoot," he said, pointing his weapon at the man, who didn't seem to care, maybe because he was wearing armor on his upper body.

Brett didn't have that advantage and raced behind the kitchen island for protection, drawing him away from Anita as she huddled behind the couch.

Bullets slammed into the wood and quartz of the island, sending bits and chips of wood and countertop flying.

At a pause in the shooting, Brett surged to his feet and returned fire, striking the man mid-chest.

The man grunted from the force of the blow, stunned for a heartbeat, while a few feet away, his partner was still battling Mango, evening the odds.

The armored attacker fired once more, driving Brett to duck beneath the kitchen island again, but he couldn't stay there, leaving Anita unprotected.

He jumped up and fired at the second intruder's exposed legs.

One of the bullets struck home.

The intruder muttered a curse in Spanish and grabbed at the wound.

In the distance, sirens rent the night air, growing louder as they sped closer.

"Vamanos," the wounded man shouted at his partner and trained his gun on Mango to free him from her powerful hold.

Fearing Mango would be hurt, Brett instructed the pit bull to release the man and come to him. *"Pust*, Mango, *Pust. K noze."*

In a blur of white and tan, his dog raced to his side and behind the protective barrier of the island.

The two men, realizing their mission had failed, scurried back out through the broken remains of the door.

Brett zoomed toward the couch to make sure Anita hadn't been injured.

She cowered close to the floor, clutching the burner phone. She gazed up at him, eyes wide, her face white with fear. In a stuttering whisper, she said, "I—I—I c-c-called 911."

"You did good," he said, holstering his weapon, and held out a hand to help her up.

She grasped his hand and, once on her feet, launched herself into his arms. "You're okay," she said, hugging him hard.

"I am and so are you, thanks to Mango," he said, and at the

mention of her name, the dog, who had followed him over, bumped their legs with her head.

He released Anita and bent to examine Mango, worried about the blows the intruder had inflicted. "You okay, girl?" he asked as he examined the pittie.

Mango sat and licked his hand as he ran it across her head.

Pounding on the front door had him back on his feet.

"Police. Open the door," someone shouted.

He hurried to the front door and peered through the peep-hole. Satisfied that it was the police, he opened the door and stepped back, hands raised as if in surrender so that they would see he was not reaching for the gun he had holstered at his side.

The cops rushed in, guns drawn. "Hands up. Keep them up there where we can see them," the one cop shouted. He planted a hand in the middle of Brett's chest and forced him back against the wall while his partner reached over and re-moved Brett's gun from the holster and tucked it into his waist-band at the small of his back.

Mango, who had moved with him to the door, growled at the cop, forcing Brett to command the dog to sit. "*Sedni*, Mango. *Sedni*."

Anita shouted from across the width of the living room, "Stop. They're the good guys."

"I'm SBS K-9 Agent Brett Madison and this is my partner, Mango. If you let me put my hands down, I'll get my ID out of my wallet," Brett said calmly, trying to de-escalate the situation.

"Don't move," the cop said, training his gun from Brett's head to Mango's as the dog sat beside him, growling. Ready to attack.

The other officer walked over to Anita. "Are you the one who called?"

ANITA NODDED, fearing for Brett and Mango. "They are agents for South Beach Security. Brett is my bodyguard and Mango, the dog, is his partner," she said, gesturing to the pit bull.

The officer narrowed his gaze, peered at her intently and, seemingly satisfied, turned to his partner and said, "You can stand down."

His partner hesitated, still eyeballing Brett, who was several inches taller and broader, as well as Mango. Both dangers if his partner was mistaken. But then the officer reluctantly complied and holstered his weapon.

"I'm guarding Ms. Reyes because she's an eyewitness to a murder. You can call Detectives Gonzalez and Williams at Miami Beach PD to confirm," Brett said.

Turning, he slowly reached for the wallet in his back pocket with one hand, the other still held up in surrender. Once he had the wallet, he finally removed a card that he handed the cop. "Or you can call Trey Gonzalez, who runs SBS," he added.

The officer took only a quick look at the card and glanced over to where his partner stood with her. "It looks legit, Sam."

Sam—Officer Monteiro, his badge read—nodded. "Can you tell us what happened?"

"Two men shot their way into the house," Anita said and pointed toward the shattered glass of the ruined sliding door.

"Mango was able to restrain one intruder, who dropped his gun," Brett said and gestured to the weapon sitting on the wooden floor. Anita noticed that there seemed to be some blood there as well.

"What about the blood?" the officer asked, also noticing it as he walked over to examine the scene, careful not to step on any possible evidence.

"The second intruder had on body armor. I had to shoot at his leg to take him down," Brett advised, then supplied physical descriptions of the two men and pressed on. "They ran once they heard the sirens, but they had to have left a trail to their transportation. Maybe our video cams or those of the neighbors might have more info."

"We'll secure the scene until the detectives arrive," Officer Monteiro said, then walked toward Brett and returned his weapon.

Brett had no sooner holstered it when his phone started ringing. "It's Trey," he said and walked over to Anita while placing the call on speaker. Despite his calm tone, his body vibrated with tension, and he raked his fingers through the short strands of his hair almost angrily.

"What's the sitch? Are you safe?" Trey asked.

"This is a soup sandwich," Brett said, words clipped and harsh.

At her puzzled gaze, he said, "Mission has gone all ways of wrong, but we're both okay. How did they know we were here?"

"We don't know. We're still working on the first leak," Trey said, the frustration obvious in his voice and the heavy sigh that drifted across the line.

"We're moving from here, Trey. Pronto."

"Detectives won't be happy if you run. They'll want to interview you," he said.

Brett shook his head sharply. "We've got to go before these guys can regroup. I know a place that should be safe, but I need wheels," he said and scrubbed his beard with one hand, his agitation clear.

"SBS K-9 Agents Perez and Rodriguez are closest to you. They can get there in less than fifteen minutes. Roni and Williams are also on their way to work with the local PD detectives," Trey advised.

Brett met her gaze, his brown gaze filled with steely determination. "Sorry, boss, but we're not going to wait around for them. Anita is not going to get killed on my watch."

A tense silence filled the air. "We're not going to let that happen. But we need to work with the police."

"Working with people we can't trust? I won't make that mistake again," Brett replied and shook his head, lips pursed. Every line of his body radiated fury that had nothing to do with what had just happened, Anita thought.

"You wait but get ready to go to your new location. There are burner phones in the desk drawer in the bedroom. Use them for all future communications. There's a pouch there also. Take it with you and use the cash inside for all purchases," Trey instructed.

Brett relaxed, but only a little. "Roger that, Trey."

He ended the call and slipped the phone into his jeans pocket. "Pack up your things so we can head to the new location once we're done with the detectives."

"Will that do any good?" Anita asked, worried that the new place wouldn't be any safer than where they had already been.

Brett laid a hand on her shoulder and squeezed. "Do you trust me, Anita?"

Trust him? The man who had broken her heart? But the image of him putting himself in harm's way to keep her safe just moments earlier immediately replaced those thoughts.

"I trust you," she said, and he shifted his hand, wrapped his arm around her shoulders and drew her in to his strong and very capable embrace.

She wavered at first, but then relented, needing the security of his arms, fighting the rise of old emotions while at the same time telling herself he wasn't the same man she had once loved. He was harder now, not as easygoing as he had once been.

Whatever had happened before, what he clearly didn't want to happen again, had changed him.

When he shifted away slightly and met her gaze, his was dark, the melty chocolaty brown almost black. Troubled. "We need to get ready to run again."

She nodded. "I'll go pack."

BRETT WATCHED HER GO, muttered a curse and dragged a hand through his hair.

If not for Mango... I won't go there. I won't let that darkness claim me again.

He bent and rubbed the dog's ears and body, confirming yet again that the dog hadn't been seriously injured by the intruder's blows. "You're a good girl," he said, earning some doggy kisses in response.

But he had to get moving and grab what he needed to keep Anita safe.

Rushing back to his bedroom, he found the burner phones and pouch in the desk and a large empty duffel in the closet. He tucked one phone into his back pocket. The pouch and the rest of the phones went into the duffel along with the clothes Trey had bought for him.

Back in the kitchen area, he packed the laptop and filled a couple of reusable grocery bags with food, including Mango's kibble. They wouldn't be able to risk leaving the new location for supplies until he was confident they hadn't been followed.

Anita walked to meet him at the kitchen table, her things tossed into a plastic bag.

"You can put them in that duffel. There's plenty of room," he said, and she packed them as instructed.

"You've got company," the officer guarding the front door called out.

He peered past the cop to where his fellow K-9 agents Matt Perez and Natalie Rodriguez stood with their dogs, Butter, a Belgian Malinois, and Missy, a Labrador retriever.

Brett walked to the door to coordinate with his fellow agents while he waited for the detectives to arrive. As he reached them, Matt held up car keys, but as Brett went for them, Matt shifted the keys away and reminded, "Trey wants you to wait for the detectives. Full police cooperation."

"I know. I don't like it, but that's what the boss wants," Brett confirmed.

"Trey needs to keep things chill with the LEOs," Natalie said.

Brett understood. SBS often worked in connection with

local law enforcement, and they had to keep a good working relationship with them. But that didn't change one very important thing on this assignment.

"I'm sure it's a cop who's leaking our safe house info."

Matt and Natalie shared a look, and then nodded in unison.

"We agree, but we cooperate for now while we work on this case," Natalie said, basically echoing what Matt and Trey had said earlier.

Brett looked away and shook his head. Blowing out an exasperated breath, he said, "We cooperate, but as soon as we're done, Anita and I are out of here."

"Agreed. You'll let Trey know where you're going?" Matt asked, gaze narrowed as he peered at Brett.

He nodded. "Trey and only Trey."

Natalie gestured to the driveway. "We'll secure this area, but after the detectives arrive, we'll see if they'll let us track your attacker's trail to where they had their getaway car."

"That sounds like a plan. Thanks," he said and went back inside to wait.

Wait and worry. Wait and fume about the leaks that were threatening Anita's life.

He more than most knew the danger of not knowing whom to trust. In Iraq his indecision had cost his squad two good soldiers and a young child's life as well. The memories of their deaths still haunted him. He wouldn't repeat that mistake again. Especially since it was Anita's life at stake. He gazed over to where she sat on the couch, waiting for the detectives to arrive.

Chapter Nine

He reminded her of a caged tiger at the zoo, pacing back and forth across the narrow width of the kitchen. It was as if he was trying to burn up the angry energy sizzling through him.

The two officers gave him plenty of room, as if sensing that he was on the knife's edge of keeping control, and it once again struck her just how different he was from the man she'd once loved.

That man was still there. She'd seen glimpses of him in the gentle way he'd been caring for her, from making an omelet to the way he'd held her, as if she was something precious.

But now a hard veneer made of danger and anger had slipped over him, two emotions she'd rarely seen from him before.

It made her wonder again what had caused the change and if it was for the better. Or maybe that facade was what he needed to work for SBS. She'd seen something similar in his boss. Hard and in control but also caring and protective, especially around his wife, Roni.

Brett met her gaze for the briefest moment, and she glimpsed the caring there, but also fear.

He hadn't wanted to wait, worried that every second they lingered at the no-longer safe house presented danger.

Luckily, the detectives for the local police force arrived and peppered first Brett and then her with questions about the attack. Sometimes they asked the same thing in different ways, as if trying to trip them up, but they remained consistent even as she could feel Brett's rising anger, like lava getting ready to spew out of a volcano.

When he scrubbed his fingers across his hair for like the tenth time in the last ten minutes, she laid a hand on his arm to hopefully ratchet down his growing exasperation.

"I think that's about all the information we can provide, detectives. I'm sure Detectives Gonzalez and Williams can give you more details about this case once they arrive, so if you don't mind, we'll be going," she said in that sweet and very polite way her Miami mother had taught her.

And she didn't wait for their approval, knowing it was unlikely to come.

She just marched to where they had made a pile of their clothing and supplies, grabbed as many bags as she could and made a beeline for the front door.

Brett chuckled beneath his breath and followed her lead.

As they bolted past the officer stationed at the front door and rushed to where Natalie and Matt stood guard by their SUVs, he murmured, "That took *guts*, Anita."

"Why, thank you, Brett," she said with a laugh.

"You two good?" Matt asked, bewilderment on his features as Brett opened the back hatch and began loading the bags.

"Could be better, but we'll survive. Thanks for all your help," Brett said and shook his hand and Natalie's.

"Anytime. We kept the perimeter clear of any lookie-loos. Hopefully no one got any info they could use to track you," Natalie replied and quickly added, "As soon as Roni and her partner get here, we'll try to follow the blood trail to see what we can get on your attackers."

"Roger. Send that info when you can," Brett said and held the passenger door open for Anita to hop into the SUV.

He harnessed Mango into the back seat, got behind the wheel and plugged an address into the GPS.

"Where are we going?" she asked as he drove out of the development.

"A marine buddy has a place down in Key Largo. He's a skier so he's normally up north at this time of year and lets me use the place if I want to get away," he said and shot a quick look at her. "It should be safer than any police or SBS locations."

"Should be?" she repeated, not liking the uncertainty of those words.

His hands tightened on the wheel, knuckles white from the pressure he was exerting.

"Only Trey will have the address, so I know it won't get leaked."

"You don't think he'll tell Roni?" They were married after all, she thought.

BRETT PURSED HIS LIPS, giving it some consideration before he said, "I think they can separate business from the personal."

Or at least I hope so.

In the months he'd been working for Trey, he'd realized that SBS wasn't just a business, it was family as well. From the top down, the employees were all either family or an extended part of the Gonzalez clan. Even some recent clients had become relations by virtue of becoming involved with the SBS K-9 agents or Gonzalez family members.

That realization had him shooting a quick glance at Anita and wondering if somehow that would be possible for them.

Until he reminded himself that he had to keep this all business and avoid any distractions that could jeopardize her life.

He dragged his gaze away from her, giving his full attention to the road and keeping an eye out for anything out of the ordinary. Much as it had on the morning drive to the safe house, everything seemed in order. No one tailing them.

At least not physically.

With today's technologies, that was no longer necessary. Cell phones and tracking devices provided a digital trove of location information to those who knew how to collect that data.

SBS was always cautious about sweeping their vehicles to make sure they were clean. The burner phones also worked, although Trey, Anita and he had used their personal phones until their arrival at the Homestead location.

He was confident Sophie and Robbie, the tech geniuses at SBS, could easily use that phone data to know where they had been.

Could the bad guys be that sophisticated or was it a simple case of someone at the police department overhearing and leaking the information?

The simplest explanation, he reminded himself, only twice in one day?

The Aventura location could have been gleaned from discussions at the stationhouse, but Trey hadn't provided the Homestead address to anyone at the department, as far as he knew. Even if he had told Roni, Brett was sure she would have safeguarded it considering what had happened.

"What are you thinking?" Anita asked, and as he glanced over at her, she added, "I'm climbing the walls wondering why this is happening."

"Why is easy. You can ID a murderer, but like you, I'm also worried about how they could get the address for the SBS safe house."

Anita frowned and her head bobbled from side to side as she considered his question. "You don't think it's a leak at the police department?" she asked, clearly picking up his vibes.

"I don't. Roni wouldn't share that with anyone," he said with a nod.

She firmed her lips and looked upward, thoughtful, and asked, "What about a tracker, like an AirTag or something like that?"

"SBS sweeps for trackers on their transportation. AirTag is possible, only we didn't bring anything with us where they could have slipped it and I think we would have noticed something in a pocket."

"That leaves the cell phones, right? Is it that easy? Could someone be tracking us now?" she asked and peered out the window, searching the road.

"We've shut down our phones and they'd have to have access to telephone company data. That normally takes a warrant—"

"Unless they have someone on the inside there as well," she jumped in.

He didn't discount that someone like Tony Hollywood, if that's who was behind the attacks, was capable of that. But he didn't think even Hollywood could get that info so quickly.

"It's possible, but I'm leaning toward a leak at the police department and I'm sure Roni has taken steps to plug that leak," he said, trying to sound more confident than he was feeling.

"You were always bad at poker," she teased with a laugh and shake of her head.

He couldn't deny that. It was why he'd always avoided playing cards with his marine buddies.

"I am bad at poker, but I have to have faith that Roni and the SBS team will have our backs."

TONY HOLLYWOOD WAS more pissed than Santiago Kennedy had ever seen.

Hollywood marched back and forth across the floor of the now-empty garage of his used car dealership.

He'd cleared it out the second that Santiago had limped in with Hollywood's useless nephew beside him, cradling his arm and whining like a little girl about how the pit bull had broken it.

"Shut up, Billy," Hollywood snapped and whirled on them. "I sent the two of you to clean up this mess and you've made it even worse," he screamed, face almost blue from his rage. Veins popped out along his forehead and the sides of his thick neck, worrying Santiago that the man would stroke out.

Hollywood was a powerful man, well over six feet with thickly muscled shoulders and a massive chest barely constrained by the expensive bespoke shirts and suits he liked to wear.

"It's broke, Tony. That dog broke it," Billy whined again.

Hollywood's temper finally erupted.

He backhanded Billy across the face, nearly knocking him out of his chair. The blow left a bright red mark and an angry scrape, courtesy of the large diamond-encrusted championship football ring Hollywood wore.

Tony told everyone he'd gotten it playing on his college football team. While Tony was certainly big enough to have been a linebacker, Santiago knew he'd taken the ring in exchange for not breaking a man's legs when he didn't pay his gambling debts.

"Do you two know what the felony murder rule is?" Hollywood said, then leaned down and got nose to nose with Santiago. "Do you?" he shouted.

Tony's spittle sprayed onto Santiago's face, but he didn't flinch or say a word. That would only make Tony even madder, if that was even possible.

At his silence, Tony straightened to his full height and dragged his fingers through the hard strands of his gelled hair.

"I sent you to find out where Manny put my money, not to kill him, Santiago," Tony said.

"He saw my face, Tony. I didn't have a choice," Santiago said.

A mistake.

Tony leaned down, grabbed hold of his injured leg and dug his fingers into the wound. Pain blasted through Santiago's brain, nearly making him faint. Dark swirls danced before his vision as Tony said, "That makes me part of the murder. That gets me life in prison unless you fix this."

"I'll fix it, Tony. I swear, I'll fix it," Santiago whined, hating that he was sounding too much like Tony's gutless nephew.

"Fix it. Get rid of the girl. Find my money," Tony said with a rough dig into his leg that nearly made him vomit.

He swallowed the bile down and nodded. "I will, Tony. I just need a few more days."

"Make it right and take this little coward to the doctor. That arm looks broken," Tony said with a sneer as he glanced at his sniveling nephew. With a final annoyed huff, Tony stormed from the garage and back into the dealership showroom.

Santiago looked over at Billy's arm. Maybe it *was* at an odd angle. And he had to have someone look at his leg anyway before they went after the girl again.

Only this time he'd take out that pit bull first, so he'd have no worries while he made the man sorry for the hole in his leg.

As for the woman, he'd have some fun with her before he killed her. Payback for making his mess-up even worse.

Wrong move, wrong timing, wrong everything, Santiago thought as he slowly rose from the chair, wincing as pain shivered up his leg.

"Let's go, Billy. We've got to finish this so Tony won't finish us," he said and pounded the young man's back, part encouragement, part punishment.

Billy peered up at him, eyes wide with disbelief. "Finish me? I'm family," he whimpered and slowly got to his feet.

Santiago laughed and shook his head. "Tony's only family is money, Billy. Best you remember that," he said and limped toward the car they'd driven into the garage barely half an hour earlier after he'd called Tony to warn him about what had happened.

That's why the garage had been empty of the usual workers who'd be prepping and fixing the secondhand cars for the dealership Tony ran as a front for his assorted operations.

Operations Santiago knew a lot about. He'd made a point of learning and writing it all down. Insurance, he thought.

He might have made a mistake in taking out Ramirez, but he didn't intend to fry for it on Old Sparky.

Not alone, at least, he thought, and hopped back into the car to visit the doctor they used for situations just like this.

Once they were patched up, they'd find her, the man and his little dog, too, Santiago thought with a strangled laugh.

"What's so funny?" Billy asked.

"You. You're so funny," he said and finally drove out of the garage to finish what he'd started.

Chapter Ten

She hadn't thought it possible, but she'd fallen asleep and woken up to the views of wide-open expanses of water as Brett drove down South Dixie Highway on the way to his friend's home.

"Are we almost there?" she asked, voice husky from her short nap.

Brett smiled and shot a quick glance at her. "We're almost there. This is Barnes Sound and we'll hit Key Largo in a few miles. My friend's place is right near John Pennekamp Coral Reef State Park. Have you ever been there?"

He made it sound like he was a tour guide, and they were on vacation, but she guessed it was because he was trying not to worry her any more than she was already worried. Because of that, she said, "I've always wanted to go. I've heard there's some great snorkeling there."

"Glass-bottomed boats as well. Maybe after this is over..." His voice trailed off as even he must have realized how it sounded given their current situation.

"Maybe," she said meekly and gave her attention to the passing scenery, trying to distract herself from thoughts of the state of her life.

Water and more water. Greenery along the edges of the highway when it hit pockets of land. Every now and then she'd look back to see if anyone was following them. The highway rose over the water and then dipped down onto what she assumed was Key Largo.

More land and a highway with an assortment of businesses. Gas stations and stores catering to people who liked to scuba, snorkel or fish. The stores were fairly spread out on the road, with big patches of trees, palms and brush between them. Lots of boats, which made sense on what was a narrow spit of land surrounded by water. The Atlantic on one side and Florida Bay and the Gulf on the other.

The sign for the state park flew by and barely a few miles had passed when Brett turned off onto a small street barely wide enough for one car, much less two. A hodgepodge of houses, no two the same except for possibly the double-wide mobile homes here and there, lined the street.

Boats or boat trailers dotted the driveways of many of the homes. Front lawns struggling for life under the hot Florida sun and salt from the nearby waters were interspersed with homes where the owners had given up the fight and filled their front lawns with gravel or electric bright white shells. Overhead the fronds of palm trees swayed weakly with an offshore breeze, and holiday-loving owners had wrapped some of the trunks with Christmas lights.

She was sure that Brett, who'd grown up with snow and evergreens in New York, likely found that an incongruous picture, but having been raised in Miami, it was a familiar sight to her.

Several yards up, Brett pulled into a driveway much like many of the others, complete with an empty boat trailer. The stone crunched beneath the tires in front of the mobile home festooned with lights and a flat splash of color on the ground that she guessed might be an inflatable Santa.

"We're here," he said but held up his hand in a stop gesture. "Let me check it out first."

She waited as he exited the car and then released Mango from the back seat. Man and dog walked past a chain-link gate and approached the side door of the mobile home, where Brett punched in something on what she assumed was a digital lock.

Brett opened the door and called out, "Jake, you home?"

When there was no answer, he unclipped Mango's leash and signaled her to inspect the home.

Anita held her breath, nervous for the dog until Mango returned a few minutes later and sat at Brett's feet on the landing. Brett entered the home, hand cautiously on his holstered gun, but likewise exited a few minutes later and returned to the car.

"It's clear. Let's get settled and I'll call Trey and let him know we're good."

She wasn't sure *good* was the right word to use for their current situation. But they were alive, so she supposed that was as good as it got at that moment.

Nodding, she left the car and followed him to the back to grab their supplies. Together they entered the mobile home, which was surprisingly more spacious than she might have imagined.

The side door opened into a living room with two wing chairs, a coffee table, a couch and an entertainment center with a large-screen television. A breakfast bar with a sea-foam-colored countertop separated that area from a galley kitchen with standard stainless-steel appliances and clean white cabinets.

A glass door off to the side of the living room/kitchen led to a deck. Opposite the breakfast island were a bistro table and two chairs.

"The bedrooms are down the hall that way," Brett said with a flip of his hand to the end of the room as she laid a bag with groceries on the kitchen counter. "You can take the main bedroom at the end," he added.

She grabbed the bag with the few clothes she had and walked down the hall, pausing to peer into the guest bathroom and first bedroom, a smallish room with a window and bunk beds for kids, she supposed.

Which made her ask, "Does your friend Jake have a family?"

Brett met her at the door, his body too close to hers in the narrow space of the hallway. "No, but his sister does. She sometimes comes to visit in the summer when the kids are off from school."

She hurried from that room to the next because being so close to him had her body responding in ways she didn't want.

That room was larger with a queen bed, nightstand, dresser and small desk all in white that looked like IKEA offerings. Above the desk was artwork of a beach scene, likewise mass-produced. But the room was happy thanks to the sunlight streaming in through the window beside the desk.

"I'll take this room," Brett said, and she supposed it was partly because they'd have to go past him to get to her in the last bedroom.

The main bedroom was much like Brett's with all-white furniture that gleamed from the sunlight flooding through the window.

She tossed the plastic bag with her "clothes" onto the bed, jammed her hand on her hips and whirled to face Brett, who stood at the door, nonchalantly leaning on the doorjamb.

"What do we do now?" she asked.

IF IT HAD been years earlier, the answer would have been easy.

He would have walked over, kissed her and in no time they would have been on that comfy-looking bed, making love.

Just the thought of it had him hardening, but that was then, and this was now, and things were totally different.

He jerked a thumb in the direction of the kitchen. "I'm going to text Trey and then scope out the deck and see if Jake's boat is there. It might come in handy."

Not that he wanted to make an escape by boat, but if he

had to, he would. His dad and he would sometimes rent a boat at the Captree Boat Basin and head out to either the Great South Bay or the Atlantic. His father had always wanted to buy a boat or, as his mother had teased, a hole in the ocean you pour money into.

As Brett stepped out onto the tiny deck that somehow crammed in a small table and four chairs, he was surprised to see a very nice new Robalo 30-foot walk-around sitting on a boatlift by the dock on the canal behind the home. It had apparently replaced Jake's old fishing boat.

"Look at that, Mango," he said to the dog as she followed him out.

He whistled beneath his breath, wondering where Jake had gotten the money for such a luxury. From what he remembered of the catalogs his father always brought home, one as recently as his last Christmas trip home, a boat like this was easily over two hundred thousand dollars. Add several thousand for the power lift. It made no sense for a friend who often complained about being short on cash.

Jake's ears must have been burning since a spectral voice from the video camera by the back door said, "Dude, I thought someone broke in but then I saw it was you. Why aren't you answering your phone?"

"My phone broke. I have a new number. I'll send it to you," he replied into the speaker for the camera. He began to text Jake the number for the burner phone, but hesitated, well aware it might be a security breach. But he had trusted Jake with his life in Iraq and he still trusted him, although the expensive boat was worrying.

He texted the number and his phone rang a second later. "Hey, Jake. Sorry for not letting you know in advance that I was borrowing your place."

"No problema, dude. I'm up at Lake Placid for a snowboarding competition. Won't be back until the new year," Jake said, his voice barely audible over the noises in the background, a mix of bad bar music and boisterous shouts.

"Sounds like you're having fun," he said, keeping it chill to not tip Jake as to the actual reason for being there.

"A blast. YOLO, you know," his old friend replied.

"YOLO, *mano*. I love the new boat. When did you get that baby?" he asked, puzzled by how a friend who had only held intermittent jobs since leaving the Marines could afford it.

A long hesitation had the hackles on his neck rising. "You still there?" he pressed.

"Yeah, dude. I came into some money. That Camp Lejeune water settlement," Jake replied and for the first time ever, Brett wasn't buying it.

"I hope you and your family are okay, *mano*," he said, hoping they were all well and not suffering from the effects of the contaminated water at their old marine camp.

"We are. Nothing to worry about, dude. Enjoy yourself and have a Merry Christmas. I'll see you when I'm back in Miami," Jake said with forced merriment and hung up before Brett could ask him anything else.

For safety's sake, Brett shut off the phone to prevent anyone tracking that signal. He'd have to grab a different burner phone for future calls. He'd already texted Trey to let him know they were okay while Anita had been scoping out the bedrooms.

"Something wrong?" Anita asked as she stepped onto the deck and bent to rub Mango's head.

He could lie, but with their lives at stake, he didn't want a lie between them.

Motioning to the boat, he said, "That's a pricey toy."

"Boys with toys," Anita said with strangled laugh.

He nodded and rubbed two fingers together in a money gesture. "Yes, boys with toys, but Jake never had the cash for that kind of toy. He claims he got a Camp Lejeune settlement."

Anita narrowed her gaze and skipped it from him to the boat and back. "And you don't believe him?"

It was tough to say it about a man he'd trusted with his life on more than one occasion, but he didn't. "Jake's dad was a marine, too, and the family was stationed there when the water contamination occurred, so it's possible."

Anita digested that. "I hate to say it, but maybe SBS should check him out."

"Great minds think alike—"

"And fools seldom differ," she said, ending the quote for him.

"Better safe than sorry," he replied, dragging another rough laugh from her.

"We're just full of platitudes today, aren't we?" she said with a shake of her head, loosening a long lock of hair from the topknot she'd fashioned. It curled onto her forehead, and he reached over and tenderly tucked it back up the way he had so many times in the past.

"Thanks," she said and repeated the gesture, clearly uncomfortable with his touch.

It shouldn't have hurt, but it did. Still, he'd been the one to abandon her and couldn't blame her even as he told himself it had been for her own good.

Flipping his hand in the direction of the house, he said, "I'm going to take Mango for a walk and get the lay of the land. Please stay indoors."

THAT WOULD BE the safest thing for her to do, but Anita was tired of being cooped up in cars and houses. The inactivity provided too much time for bad thoughts to fester.

"I'd rather take the walk with you. I think I should know where to go, too, just in case."

He hesitated for a heartbeat, but then nodded. "It's a good idea."

Sweeping his hand toward the gate in the low railing that

surrounded the deck, he invited her to walk with him and Mango in that direction.

With a few short steps, Anita unlatched the gate and stepped onto the cement path that ran behind all the houses and next to the docks where boats in all sizes, shapes and colors lined a canal.

The late-afternoon sun was still strong, glaring down onto the area. She shielded her eyes with her hand as Brett asked, "Do you know how to drive a boat?"

She nodded. "My father used to take us out sometimes on weekends. Every now and then he let me be the captain."

Brett pointed eastward along the water. "At the end of the canal, take a left and head straight to Blackwater Sound and the Intracoastal Waterway."

"Good to know," she said, although she hoped that this time they wouldn't have to worry about making an escape, especially by water. Even though she'd regularly boated with her dad and sister, the vastness of the ocean oftentimes made her feel uneasy. Too alone even when surrounded by her family.

"Exit to the street is right around that corner," he said and pointed to the far side of the mobile home.

He clipped the leash on Mango, and they walked around the corner to a narrow alley that ran between the two homes. A double set of stairs ran to the side door, one leading toward the driveway and the other toward the canal and dock.

Brett opened the gate to the chain-link fence that formed a barrier between the homes in the alley and secured the side-entrance area.

Her sneakers crunched on the uneven white stone blanketing a driveway barely long enough for their large SUV.

The home was just a couple of doors down from the corner and Brett gestured with his hand in that direction and explained how to get back to the Overseas Highway in case she needed to get away.

It struck her then that he was preparing for her to go it alone, only she had no plans of doing so.

"I'm not going anywhere without you," she said.

His face hardened into a look she'd never seen before. It was a stony, impenetrable face that spoke volumes as he glanced away before slowly meeting her gaze again. She knew what he would say, and it sent a sickly chill through her body, making her stomach churn.

"You may have to."

"I'm not going anywhere without you," she repeated and laid a hand on her belly to quell the upset there.

He firmed his lips, battling to stay silent, and reluctantly nodded. Reaching out, he cradled her cheek and she leaned into that embrace, drawing comfort from his touch.

"We go together," he said and shifted his hand to wrap it around her neck and draw her into his embrace.

Less than twenty-four hours earlier she would have protested the move, but not now. Not when it was possible that they might die if they couldn't stop the attacks. That he would be willing to give up his life to keep her safe.

As she stepped out of the embrace, wiping away unexpected tears, he kept an arm around her waist and she did the same, slipping her arm around his.

Much like he'd changed emotionally, he had changed physically as well.

He'd been fit as a soldier, but much like he'd become harder emotionally, his body had become harder as well. Leaner and more dangerous, but maybe that's what he needed in this new line of work.

Well, that and Mango, she thought as the dog loped beside him, tongue dangling from her mouth until the animal looked up at her and seemed to grin. Except she had seen what that mouth could do and was happy Mango was on their side.

It was quiet on the narrow streets as they walked, the only

sounds that of the nearby oleanders and bushes rustling around them and an occasional boat engine in the distance. But as they walked the final block or two, the susurrus of passing cars intruded, warning they were close to the highway that ran from Key West all the way back up onto the mainland.

They turned and retraced their steps, stopping only to let Mango relieve herself.

It didn't take long to reach Jake's house again, but as he had before, Brett instructed her to stop by the gate while he made sure the area was still secure.

She held her breath, expectant, waiting for another attack, but seconds later Brett signaled to her that all was fine. She pushed through the gate and up the stairs into the home.

Inside the house, she flew into action, needing to stay busy to keep nasty thoughts from rooting in her brain.

Chapter Eleven

Brett watched Anita flit and flutter around the kitchen like a butterfly sampling nectar as she checked out the cupboards and fridge to see what was there.

She was already planning a menu, he could tell, and didn't interfere.

The planning would keep her busy and stop her from worrying.

What would keep him from worrying was knowing if they'd made any progress in identifying their suspect. Or maybe he should say suspects now that there were two of them working together.

Not wanting to add to Anita's worries, he walked to his bedroom and closed the door for privacy, but left it open just a gap so he could keep an ear open for any signs of trouble. When just the routine sound of pots and pans came, he called Trey.

"Good to hear from you, Brett. How's the place?" his boss asked.

"Safe. For now," Brett replied, that niggling worry about the boat ruining the peace he'd hoped to feel at Jake's place.

"What's the sitch?" Trey asked, picking up on his disquiet.

"Place is secure only… Could you do me a favor and check out something?" he said and when Trey agreed, he relayed the details about the boat, supposed settlement and Jake's real name and info. It made him feel guilty that he was doubting a friend, but he'd trusted the wrong person before with disastrous results. He refused to repeat that mistake.

"We can try to find out more," Trey confirmed.

"What about the leak? Any luck with that?"

"We've got the surveillance video from the back entrance at Miami Beach PD a short while ago. We're scanning it now," he said and quickly added, "The good news is that we think we've ID'd the initial suspect using facial recognition. I'll send you his info via email as well as several other photos for you to use in a photo lineup to show Anita."

Brett nodded. "Any connection to Hollywood?"

"Possibly. You'll see the rap sheet in the email. There's a major escalation from low-level bookmaking to assaults."

"You think he's been breaking legs for Hollywood?" Brett asked and blew out a rough breath, even more worried now that they had a more credible link to the mobster.

"Again, possibly. We may know more if the FBI ever gets back to us," Trey said, his tone filled with exasperation.

"Feds are slow-walking this. I guess they're worried the local LEOs are going to make their bust," Brett said, equally frustrated that the agents on the case would be more concerned with getting credit for the collar than keeping Anita safe.

Trey cursed the Feds and then quickly added, "We're going to get this guy. And his accomplice and Hollywood if we have to. Whatever it takes to keep you both safe."

"Agreed. Send me what you have—"

"I will. We'll have a video meeting at twenty hundred again, if that's good," Trey said.

With a shake of his head and rough laugh, Brett said, "I'll check my dance card and see if I'm free."

A troubled chuckle skipped across the phone before Trey signed off with, "Watch your six."

SANTIAGO SLOWED THE car they'd "stolen" from Hollywood's used car lot. If they got into trouble with it, they'd let Hollywood's manager know so he could report it missing to provide cover.

Police were still crawling all over the Homestead location. If Anita and the SBS agent were coming back here, it wouldn't be for some time.

"Why are we here?" Billy asked from beside him and gestured toward the house. His cast banged on the window, drawing the attention of an eagle-eyed cop at the curb, forcing Santiago to quickly drive away.

"You're a jerk," he said.

Billy glanced at him blankly and repeated his question. "Why? You think they'd be foolish enough to come back here?"

"Have you ever seen a rabbit on a trail when they're being hunted by a dog?" he asked.

Billy shook his head. "Do I look like I hunt rabbits?"

The Brooklyn was thick in his voice, picked up from his parents despite a lifetime in Miami.

Using one hand while keeping the other on the wheel, he mimicked Billy's accent as he said, "Rabbits will double back on a trail and wait for the dog to rush by, chasing the scent. As soon as the dog is far enough away, the rabbit will take off in the opposite direction."

"You think they're going to be rabbits and come back?" Billy said, eyes widening as the dim light bulb in his head went off as he finally understood.

"Maybe," Santiago said and pulled away to head back toward the Aventura location, another place they might rabbit to.

"What if they don't?" Billy pressed.

"If they don't, we'll find them some other way. Your uncle has a lot of connections," Santiago replied, thinking about the cop feeding them info as well as the many marks who owed Hollywood in one way or another.

A long silence followed, and Santiago could swear that he smelled wood burning. Flipping a quick glance in Billy's direction, the boy's troubled expression made his gut tighten with worry.

"What's up, Billy?"

Billy glanced at him and nervously plucked at a thread in a tear in his jeans. "Is it true what my uncle said? You know, about that rule thing?"

"The felony murder rule?" Santiago asked, just to make sure he was understanding Billy's concerns.

"Yeah, that thing," Billy said, sounding way younger than his twenty years.

Santiago understood his worry. Billy still had a lot of life to live and doing it behind bars was a scary thought.

Just as it was for him since he was only a decade older than Billy.

"It's true," he said, prompting Billy's immediate objection.

"But I didn't kill anyone. You shot Manny and the cops," he shouted, nervous sweat erupting on his upper lip as he pounded his uninjured hand on his thigh in agitation.

"It doesn't matter, Billy. You were there. You're as much a part of it as I am," he said steadily, trying to calm the increasingly agitated young man.

Waving his arms, his cast banging on the door and window again, Billy cried, "I won't go down for this. I won't. I didn't do it."

Billy was right that he hadn't pulled the trigger.

I did, and I'll be the one going to Old Sparky if Billy talks.

Which meant there was one more thing he had to do.

Like he'd thought before, Tony Hollywood only had one family: money.

He'd never miss a coward like Billy.

COOKING SOOTHED HER as it always did.

Since Brett had mentioned it, she busied herself making

the *arroz con pollo* that he had said he loved while he worked at the nearby breakfast bar.

Much like he'd said he'd loved you, the little voice in her head chastised.

Trey had bought chicken breasts, which could get too dry, so she browned them quickly and removed them from the pot with the onions, peppers, garlic and pepperoni. She'd had to substitute pepperoni for the chorizo she normally used and hoped it wouldn't change the flavor too drastically.

She added the rice to coat it with the oil and keep the rice from clumping as it cooked.

Tomato sauce came next along with oregano, bay leaves, salt and pepper. She covered the Dutch oven and slipped it into the preheated oven. Once the rice was further along, she'd add the chicken breasts and finish the meal.

Which meant she had at least fifteen minutes or so before she had to do anything else.

Walking over to Brett, she swept a hand across his shoulders and asked, "Anything new?"

Beneath her hand his muscles tensed. "SBS has some photos of possible suspects. Want to take a look?"

His tension transferred itself to her.

I want to look, but then I don't want to also. What if it isn't him in the photos, but then what if it is?

"Yes, I want to see," she finally said and plopped onto the stool beside Brett.

Slightly turning the laptop in her direction, he brought up an array of photos. All of the men had comparable looks and hair. Anita scoured the assorted faces, worried that they all had such similar features, but there was one man who stuck out.

She pointed to his photo and said, "That's him. I'm sure that's him."

Brett nodded and enlarged the photo from the suspect's rap sheet.

Anita narrowed her gaze, inspecting the photo more carefully. The jaw was the same, but the hair was different. Longer. Darker she supposed, although with the buzz cut he now had, hair color was hard to tell. What cinched it for her were the eyes, those dark, almost soulless eyes, and the small scar beneath the one.

"That's definitely him."

Brett nodded and zoomed in to show his name. "Santiago Kennedy. Teen records are sealed, but he was arrested at twenty for bookmaking. Pled it down from a five-year stretch to two and got off in one for good behavior."

"Isn't there legal gambling in Florida? Why do people still use bookies?" she asked, surprised by that.

"Florida still has a lot of restrictions on sports gambling and bookies don't do a credit check because gamblers know what happens if you don't pay."

Like Manny had paid.

A frisson of fear skipped down her spine. She pointed to the laptop and asked, "Is that it? Is that all he's done?"

Brett shook his head. "There are later arrests. Mostly misdemeanor assault and battery arrests. In a few cases the victims recanted, probably worried about retribution or losing the use of their bookie."

"So he just walks the streets, a free man? Free to kill Manny and me? Free to shoot all those cops," she said, frustration giving rise to anger.

"Not once we're done with him. We will wrap up this case so tight there will be no way for him to get free again," Brett said and placed an arm around her shoulders. Hugged her to him and dropped a kiss on her temple as he whispered, "We will get him."

"And his accomplice. But what about Tony Hollywood?" Anita asked, worried that there would be no safe place until they somehow had him in custody as well.

"If anyone can connect the dots to Hollywood, it's SBS." There was no hesitation in his voice, tempering her anger and frustration. Bringing some calm, especially as he said, "I smell something tasty. Is it what I think it is?"

She smiled and nodded. "It is. My way of saying thanks for everything."

Not that chicken and rice was any kind of payback for risking his life for her.

BRETT APPRECIATED THE gesture that could rouse so many memories. It had always been a special meal between them. And maybe it was time to put things to rights about what had happened so many years earlier.

"Thank you and… I know it's probably too late to say this, but I'm sorry for what happened between us. I truly am."

Her body did a little jump of surprise and then relaxed. "What did happen, Brett? Why did you ghost me?"

Thoughts whirled through his brain, so many, so quickly until he found himself blurting out, "Maybe because I felt like a ghost myself."

Her eyes opened wide with shock, and she tried to speak, her mouth opening and closing several times before she finally managed a stifled, "Why?"

Why? As if I haven't asked myself that hundreds, maybe thousands of times.

He shrugged and looked away, struggling to find the words as he had so many times before when others had asked. His commanding officer. A therapist. Trey, although he'd managed to unload some of it on his old friend because he had trusted him to understand.

She cradled his jaw and applied gentle pressure until he met her concerned gaze. "Why?" she repeated, patiently, like a parent coaxing a child to share a bad dream.

I only wish it had been a bad dream.

But like bad dreams that became less scary when you shared them, maybe it was time to let her in on what had happened.

"There was a young Muslim boy who used to hang out near our camp when we were deployed in Iraq. He was fascinated by my dog because some Muslim sects don't allow dogs as pets. They consider them unclean," he began, then paused to take a shaky breath before pressing on.

"I tried not to get involved with him, but he kept on tagging along and eventually he was a regular. He loved playing with Rin Tin Tin—"

"Rin Tin Tin? Really?" she said with a laugh.

He chuckled and shook his head. "Yeah, someone thought it would be funny for a German shepherd to be named Rin Tin Tin. Anyway, Yusef—that was the boy's name—asked to play with Rin—that's what I would call him—and I broke down and let him."

He had to stop then as the memories rose up, as powerful as the day it had happened. His chest tightened and his heart hammered so hard and fast it echoed in his ears. Sucking in a deep breath, he held it in, fighting for control.

Anita leaned toward him and laid a hand on his as it rested on the tabletop. "It's okay if you want to stop."

He released the breath in a steady, controlled stream and shook his head. "No, it's time. I want you to understand," he said and twined his fingers with hers.

"I'm here for you," she said, her gaze fixed on his face.

"Because we knew Yusef, trusted Yusef, we didn't think anything of it when he came into camp one morning."

Pausing, he looked away from her and forced himself to continue. "I should have seen something was off with him. I'm supposed to see things like that. Rin saw it. He was agitated, barking and jerking at his leash."

The images slammed into him almost as powerfully as the

blast that day, stealing his breath. Tightening the muscles in his throat, choking him into silence.

The reassuring squeeze of Anita's hand on his provided welcome comfort and support. When he met her gaze, the understanding there nearly undid him. Somehow, he finished.

"The local ISIS group knew Yusef had access to the camp. They'd rigged him with a suicide vest filled with explosives. Punishment for us and him since he'd played with Rin."

"You can't blame yourself for what happened," she urged, her gaze sheened with tears, her voice thick with her own upset.

"I can. Like I said, I should have seen it. By the time I realized Rin had picked up on the explosives, it was too late. The blast tore through the camp, killing two members of my squad and injuring another half a dozen."

Chapter Twelve

"You and Rin? Were you hurt?" Anita asked, worried Brett would downplay his own wounds, both physical and emotional.

With a quick shrug and jerk of his head, he said, "We were luckier than most. Luckier than my two friends and Yusef. He was only ten. Those savages sacrificed a child."

She let that sink in and realized that he didn't really think he'd been lucky that day. That he carried the heavy burden of not only survivor's guilt, but also doubt about his instincts. About whom he could trust.

Maybe that was the emotional hardness she sensed. The wall he'd built around himself.

"Is that why you stopped writing and calling?" she asked.

He looked away again, but she cradled his jaw and urged him to face her. "Is it?" she pressed.

"What we had was...so special. After what happened, I didn't feel I deserved something like that. Something the two soldiers who'd died that day and Yusef would never get to have because of me," he said, his voice breaking with the emotion he was barely keeping in check.

Tapping his chest, directly over his heart, he said, "I couldn't trust myself not to make wrong choices again. Choices that hurt the people I care about. Like now. I can't let feelings get in the way of what I have to do. I have to stay focused."

Anita had never been a patient person, but cooking had

taught her that very important virtue. You couldn't rush a dish if you wanted it to come out right.

Much like she couldn't rush this if she wanted him to be okay with his past. If she wanted things to be good between them.

After all, no matter his reasons, this man had left her without a word. And he wasn't the same man she'd once loved. He was different, and he was right that if they were going to get out of this situation alive, they couldn't let emotions distract them.

She dropped her hand from his face and untwined her fingers from his. "You're right. We need to keep level heads to finish this," she said, her voice as calm and supportive as she could muster.

He nodded and scrubbed his face with his hands. When he met her gaze again, the hard man was back. The stony look had returned and all emotion had been wrestled back inside.

For a moment she regretted that this man had reappeared, remembering the man she'd loved and who had emerged briefly to share his wounds.

But then the ding-ding-ding of the timer she'd set registered, calling her to action.

She shoved away from the table and back to the kitchen where she took out the Dutch oven, stirred the rice and nestled the chicken breasts in the rice to finish cooking.

At the breakfast bar, Brett had resumed work, his concentration on his laptop, although as she prepped the final toppings for the chicken and rice and an avocado salad, she caught him occasionally glancing in her direction. She told herself it wasn't longing she saw in that gaze. It was just worry about this case and their safety.

Armed with that conviction because it would protect her heart, she puttered around in the kitchen, cleaning and keeping busy until another timer warned dinner was ready.

Anita pulled the chicken and rice out of the oven and, satisfied it was finished, she called out to Brett, "I'm going to set the table."

He immediately closed the laptop and hopped up. "Let me do that. I'm sure you have things to finish."

She did and welcomed his assistance as he grabbed place mats from a nearby cabinet, cutlery from a drawer and napkins from a holder on the kitchen counter.

While he set the table, she spooned chicken and rice onto the plates and topped the servings with roasted red peppers she had made from a wrinkly pepper she had found wasting away in the fridge. Frozen sweet peas nuked in the microwave completed the dish.

She set those plates on the table, returned to the kitchen for the avocado salad and placed that on the table as well.

"There's some beer if you'd like, and it's not skunky. I used one of the bottles for the *arroz con pollo*," she said with a dip of her head in the direction of the fridge.

A BEER SOUNDS like heaven, Brett thought, and only one wouldn't affect his judgment in the event something happened tonight. Although he hoped for the first quiet night in days.

"Thanks. A beer would be great," he said and sat in front of a heaping plate of chicken and rice.

She set a beer in front of him and nervously wiped her hands on the apron she wore. "I normally would make *maduros* with this, but we didn't have any."

He loved sweet, ripe plantains, but understood their supplies were limited. "Maybe if things stay quiet, we can do some shopping tomorrow for food and clothing."

"That would be nice. I know Trey meant well, but something besides T-shirts and sweats would be good," she said with a half smile and tug at the oversize T-shirt she wore.

"I'll work it out with Trey," he said, and once she'd sat, he dug into the meal.

The flavors burst in his mouth, as delicious as he remembered. Maybe better, he thought and murmured in appreciation. "This is delicious."

"Thanks. I had to make do with what I had," she said, obviously uneasy as she picked at the meal she'd prepared.

"Well, you did good, Reyes. Real good," he teased and forked up a healthy portion of the chicken and rice.

HIS PRAISE LIGHTENED her mood, and they both must have been hungry since they ate in companionable silence. She was grateful for that because it kept away worry about the fact someone was trying to kill her as well as the conflicting emotions she had for Brett.

They finished the meal and cleaned up with little said, falling into the patterns they'd shared when they'd been together. After, he fed Mango, gave her fresh water and they took her for a quick walk.

Nightfall had come quickly in early December, but there was enough illumination on the street from the nearby homes, Christmas lights and scattered streetlamps. By the time they returned from the short walk, the puddled color that sprawled in the driveway by the mobile home had inflated. A large bare-chested Santa in board shorts, complete with a surfboard, greeted them upon their return.

"I gather Jake is quite a character," she said and chuckled.

"He is. You could always count on Jake to liven things up," he said and laughed, but then grew serious, his look severe and troubled.

She laid a hand on his arm. "I know you're bothered by that boat, but maybe there's a reasonable explanation."

"Maybe," he said and held up his hand to stay her entry as he went through the process that was becoming almost familiar by now. He entered through the side gate, opened the house and sent in Mango. Once Mango had given the "all clear," Brett signaled for Anita to follow.

Inside they each hurried to what had become their domains. Brett sat at the breakfast bar with the laptop, preparing for their upcoming meeting. She went to the kitchen to make coffee, expecting that it would be another late night.

By the time the coffee was sputtering in the espresso pot, Brett's laptop was chiming to warn it was time for their video meeting.

The television across the way from them snapped to life with the image of the SBS crew sitting around the table at their Brickell Avenue office. Roni and her partner were also there, faces solemn.

She worried whether that meant good or bad news but didn't press. They'd share when they were ready.

At the table, she set down the cups of coffee and took a spot beside Brett.

He mouthed a "thank you."

Trey began the meeting. "I'm sure Brett has shared the photo lineup with you," he said and displayed the array of photos she had seen earlier onto the screen. "Can you identify any of them as the man you saw the night Ramirez was murdered?"

Anita nodded and used the touch pad on the laptop to move the mouse until it rested on the photo she had picked out earlier.

"I'm sure that's the man," she said, and Trey returned the screen to the team. He handed Roni a piece of paper.

She nodded and said, "I hope this photo lineup will fly with the district attorney."

"Why wouldn't it?" Anita asked, puzzled.

"We would have preferred to do it ourselves, but there are exigent circumstances obviously. It would also be better if we could wait for the DNA analysis from the blood at the Homestead location," Roni said.

Williams quickly added, "Florida started collecting DNA in 2011 so Kennedy's DNA should be in the system because of his priors."

BUT DNA ANALYSIS could take time. *Time we don't have*, Brett thought.

"What about the leak? Trey mentioned earlier that you have video that might help?" he pressed.

Trey motioned for Sophie to take over, and a second later, a video popped up on the screen.

A uniformed officer, cap pulled low and his head tucked down, walked past the SBS SUV parked at the back entrance, paused and took a long look at the vehicle. He did another walk back and forth before entering the stationhouse again.

As he did so, he tipped his head down to avoid showing his face to the camera.

"We're working up his approximate size and weight so Roni and Heath can look through the database of officers at the stationhouse," Sophie said.

"How long will that take?" he pressed.

"Our end will be relatively quick thanks to John's supercomputer, but the police analysis may take a little time since we can't access their database," Robbie advised.

Brett slumped back in his chair and released a frustrated sigh. "Doesn't seem like we have much."

Roni quickly countered with, "Actually, we think that this officer memorized your license plate number in order to track you."

Anita leaned forward in interest and said, "Track us? With just the plate number?"

Roni and Williams shared an uneasy look and Williams finally explained, "PD has a number of automatic license plate readers in police cars as well as in static locations in Miami and along Route 1, which you took to reach Homestead. There's also a database of ALPRs from HOAs and other private places that feed info into a database we can access."

"And did someone access it?" Anita pushed.

"It will take time, but we're working to see who accessed the info," Roni confirmed with a tilt of her head.

Anita's rising tension coupled with his frustration seemed obvious since Trey said, "We're working this as fast as we can, Anita."

Brett believed that, but again, it was time they might not have if Hollywood and his crew had a say. Which made him ask, "What about Hollywood? Have you made a link to him?"

"Nothing yet, but we're—"

"Working on it," Anita finished, her irritation obvious.

"We are. Other than coincidence about the bookmaking and assaults, probably to secure payment of gambling debts, we don't have a direct link but we will," Trey confirmed, his tone brooking no disagreement. "If there's nothing else," he said.

Brett and Anita did a quick glance at each other and were clearly in silent agreement. "Nothing else. I'll keep working on whatever I can find out about our suspect," Brett said.

"We'll keep you advised as soon as we have more," Trey said and a second later the video feed ended.

Brett reached out and laid a hand on Anita's shoulder, squeezed lightly to offer reassurance. "I know it seems like there's not much progress, but you shouldn't worry."

She bit her lower lip and glanced away, but he didn't press. When she finally looked back, she said, "I'm worried about my business. My life." Pointing between the two of them, she said, "Us."

He wanted to say there was no "us" now, only it would be a lie. From the moment he'd laid eyes on her at the police station, all the old feelings and emotions had awoken. Denying them would be a lie and, as he'd thought before, he didn't want any lies between them.

Mimicking her gesture, he said, "This 'us' is complicated and dangerous right now, as we discussed."

She nodded, in agreement, and shifted the conversation to a safer topic. "Do you think I can call my sous-chef in the morning? My parents too?"

"As long as you use a burner phone. I'll get you one first thing tomorrow."

THE MORNING COULDN'T come fast enough as far as Anita was concerned.

Although she'd busied herself to keep distracted, with the meeting done and the evening looming large in front of her, it was impossible not to think about how her restaurant's lunch service had gone, whether the promised porterhouse steaks had arrived and how the dinner service was faring. By now it would be in full swing, and while she itched to call, waiting made sense.

She worried that even with a burner phone they'd be able to track them.

"Can you track a 'burner phone'?" she asked, using air quotes for emphasis.

Brett nodded. "You can track *any* phone. That's why we try to keep phone use to a minimum."

"And what about those APRs or whatever? Do you think they could have used that to track us to here?" she pressed.

Chapter Thirteen

"ALPRs," he corrected and jumped back on his laptop. "If they somehow grabbed Matt's license plate number, which I'm confident they didn't, they might be able to track it. There's a public site that may have more info," he said and popped up the video feed from the laptop to the television again.

Anita stood and walked closer to the television to get a better look as Brett typed in the zip code for Miami and chose a camera type. The website populated with a bunch of brown dots to show where various kinds of cameras were located. ALPRs, red light and speed cameras were all noted on the map.

"This is a crowd-sourced database so it relies on users providing this information," he said and used the mouse to move the map and display where ALPRs might have been on their route.

Relief flooded her as she realized the last location was in Homestead and the areas beyond that were clear of any readers until Big Pine Key, which she believed was quite a distance south of them.

"We're clear," she said with a happy sigh.

"Looks that way. Time for you to relax and get some rest. If things have settled down in the morning, you can make your call and we'll take that drive for supplies."

"That sounds good. I'm going to shower," she said and jerked a thumb in the direction of the bedrooms.

A shower, together with the info they'd just uncovered, would help her relax.

"WHAT DO YOU mean Billy took off?" Tony Hollywood roared, fists clenched, face mottled with angry red and sickly white.

Santiago held his hands out in pleading. "He freaked out when you mentioned the felony murder rule. Started crying like a little baby about how he was too young to go to prison for life. He said he needed a refill for that stupid vape thing he's always sucking on and went into the store but never came out."

"Find him. Check with my sister. Billy was always a mama's boy," Tony said and marched over. Jabbing a finger into Santiago's chest, so hard he was sure he'd have bruises, Tony said, "If he's a weak link, I need to know so we can deal with him."

"Deal with him? How?" Santiago asked, sure of what Tony would say, which was why he was surprised when his boss responded with, "Just find him and bring him here. I could always talk some sense into the kid. Besides, he's family."

Santiago cursed silently, hating that he'd been so wrong about what Tony would do to Billy, because if the truth came out...

"I'll find him, Tony. I'm sure he's just chilling somewhere and licking his wounds."

"What about the girl? Any news?" Tony asked, raising a hairy eyeball in a way that had Santiago sweating a bit.

"We lost them after they left Homestead, but I'm working on it," he said, hoping his connection at the police station could point them in the right direction again.

Tony grunted. "Make it happen. Yesterday, Santiago. And find Billy before he does something stupid."

He nodded and rushed from the room, a streak of curses escaping him as he realized he was in deep trouble.

Family meant something to Tony. He'd made a big mistake and there was possibly only one way to rectify that error.

Find the girl before the police found Billy. Or what was left of him anyway.

BRETT HAD GROWN frustrated at the dead ends he'd been hitting for information on Tony Hollywood.

Sure, there were a bunch of news articles and reports on the mobster, but nothing that could link him to a low-level criminal like Santiago Kennedy.

Wanting a fresh set of eyes, he'd taken a break to shower, and come out to find Anita stretched out on the couch in a fresh T-shirt and sleeping shorts.

He needed time to think about all that was happening and what they had so far in the investigation and stepped out onto the small deck, with Mango at his side. The night was peaceful, the only sounds those of the palm fronds moving overhead, a distant set of wind chimes and the canal waters lapping up against the nearby wooden dock and bulkhead.

There were lights on here and there in the homes along the canal. Some people even had Christmas lights strung along their docks and boats. The reflections of the colors created a watercolor-like kaleidoscope on the surface of the canal.

A few houses down, a bright green light in the water highlighted the shadows of snook attracted by the glow so a fisherman might snag them for a meal.

He'd caught more than one himself when Jake and he had fished from this dock.

Jake.

He hadn't asked about his friend during the video meeting, thinking it had likely been too soon for Trey to have any info. Plus, he wanted to believe for as long as possible that he could trust Jake.

Mango nudged his leg and glanced up at him, eyes almost sad, as if she sensed Brett's upset.

He knelt and rubbed the dog's head and ears, accepted the doggy kisses some people he'd met would think of as impure. In his mind, nothing connected to love was impure, but to each their own.

"Let's do a last walk," he said, even if the walk only consisted of a quick check around the house and the immediate area.

Since it would be a short stroll, he didn't bother clipping a leash on Mango. He just stuffed a fresh poop bag into his pocket and, without a word, the dog heeled to his side, breaking their connection only long enough to relieve herself. Brett cleaned up the waste and deposited it in a trash can in the side yard.

Thankfully there was nothing to see in and around the perimeter of the house.

With it all quiet, he went back inside to find Anita asleep in front of the television. A gentle snore escaped her every now and then, signaling she was in deep sleep.

He'd wake her if he shut off the television. He only turned down the volume, so he'd be able to hear any abnormal noises. Returning to his laptop, he fired it up and got back to work, intending to search for anything he could find on Tony Hollywood or Santiago Kennedy.

Jake.

He hated that he had to add his friend to the mix, but he couldn't risk any surprises.

He made a hand gesture to Mango to take a spot by the back door and the dog immediately obeyed, stretching out her tan-and-white body across the entrance. Her large, squarish head rested on her paws.

With Mango on guard, he gave his attention to the internet searches and found Kennedy on social media. More than once their suspect had bragged about his guns and connections but never mentioned Hollywood. It made him wonder why the posts with the weapons weren't flagged when so many other, less dangerous posts sometimes put a user in social media jail.

Brett took screenshots of the posts and saved the links to a list to share with Trey and the team. He suspected one of those guns could be the same make and caliber as the one used to shoot Ramirez and the police officers.

But as he was about to flip away from Kennedy's profile, something snagged his attention: a series of photos taken at a racetrack.

Checking the time stamps, he realized it was while the Paloma Challenge had been held. He screenshotted those and saved the links as well, and just to confirm, he pulled up photos of Waterside Park.

Bingo, he thought. The background in Kennedy's photo was Waterside Park, confirming that Kennedy had been at the racetrack at the same time as Ramirez.

Of course, that coincidence alone wasn't enough to say any wrongdoing had occurred at the track. Unless they could get more info, it was just coincidence.

The Feds might have more details, but clearly they didn't want to share. Keeping it to themselves could be about not having their case blown, but it could also be about not losing the collar of a high-profile criminal like Tony Hollywood to a bunch of local cops. Or SBS, for that matter.

Checking the dates on the races, he realized that a few months had gone by. Probably too long a time for anyone to be holding on to CCTV tapes, but you didn't have an event like that without plastering it all over social media to get the most bang for your buck. Not to mention local news stories as well.

Locating the page for the event, he scrolled through the photos leading up to the big occasion and then race day itself. Most of the photos were of the horses, jockeys and all the beautiful people and entertainers who would be there. Interspersed with them were a few screenshots of the crowd.

He zipped right past one crowd photo, but something called him back to it.

Was it just wishful thinking that the two people way in the

back, in the fuzzy section of the photo, looked like Ramirez and Kennedy?

As he had before, he did a screenshot and saved the link. This time he also downloaded the photo since Kennedy had made his profile public. *Clearly not a rocket scientist*, he thought.

Brett's own page was limited to family and private because you never knew who might be trying to find you. Like now.

The resolution of the picture wasn't good to begin with, but he still tried to enhance the fuzzy section with his very basic photo editing software. That served to convince him that he wasn't imagining it.

It certainly looked like Ramirez and Kennedy although they were both wearing hats, which hid their hair and could alter their overall look.

Still, it was worth sending that info to Sophie and Robbie. If anyone could work magic on that blurry photo, it would be them.

Satisfied that he had added one more dot to connect Ramirez's killer to Tony Hollywood, he did the one thing that he was dreading.

He pulled up Jake's social media and delved through all the posts and photos.

The latest ones confirmed that he wasn't lying about being in Lake Placid and a snowboarding competition. There was photo after photo of him with other snowboarders on the slopes. Some of Jake racing posted by the event organizers. Others with the groupies who tagged after a good-looking and charming guy like Jake.

He scrolled through the timeline, searching for anything about the boat.

Nothing.

That didn't make sense since most people who got their hands on a toy like that were likely to post photos of their new baby.

Unless you didn't want people to know, which seemed odd, especially for his friend.

Jake had always been someone who put everything out there. He'd never had anything to hide...until now.

He hadn't been wrong to think there had been hesitation when he'd asked Jake about the boat.

Growing suspicions curled their way around his gut, making him feel sick. Making him worry that he'd made a mistake again to trust his old friend.

It was that worry that drove him to pick up his phone to call Trey even though it was nearly midnight. But if he knew Trey, his friend and boss was probably still at work as well. Just in case, especially since Roni would likely be asleep, he texted him first.

You up?

Yes. Still at the office. Give me a minute. Roni's on my couch.

Because he also didn't want to wake Anita, he tiptoed to his bedroom and closed the door, but left it slightly ajar to listen for any issues.

"What's up?" Trey said after Brett answered.

"I may have found a connection between Ramirez and Kennedy. I emailed you a photo from the racetrack. I think it's them in the background."

"Good work. Every little piece of the puzzle helps," Trey said.

"What about the Feds? Still nothing?" Brett asked.

A rough sigh sputtered across the line. "Nada. They're not good at playing well with others."

"What about the cop in the video? Anything?" he pressed.

"Williams went back to the station with the info Sophie and Robbie provided about his physical description. Plus, Williams thought there was something familiar about the cop, so hopefully we'll know more soon," Trey advised, but Brett picked up something in his old friend's voice. Something that had nothing to do with the case.

"You good?" he asked, concerned about his friend.

"Roni isn't feeling well. It's why she didn't go back to the station with Williams," Trey replied.

Roni was the love of his life. He'd never expected to see that with a hard-ass like Trey, but Fate had apparently had other plans for his friend.

"Take care of her first, Trey. She and the baby are what's most important."

Another sigh filled the line. A tired one this time. "They are. I've got the others on double to get things moving. We'll work on that photo ASAP."

"Thanks, Trey. I'll keep on working on this, too," he said.

"I know you will," Trey replied and ended the call.

"Is everything okay?" Anita asked as she opened the door to the bedroom.

As Anita peered at him, Brett schooled his features, forcing away his fears about Roni but also about Anita and what he was feeling for her.

The devastation he'd feel if he somehow lost her after finding her once again.

Chapter Fourteen

Brett was standing in the room, his face in partial shadow from the dim light cast by a small bedside lamp. But despite that, it was impossible to miss the sorrow in his dark gaze as he said, "Trey is worried because Roni isn't feeling well."

"Is she going to be okay?" she asked, likewise worried because the woman was fairly far along in her pregnancy.

He did a quick jerk of his shoulders and ran his fingers across the short strands of his hair. "I hope so. She had some issues a few months ago but was doing better."

"Is she in the hospital?" she asked, and Brett quickly shook his head.

"Just resting at the SBS offices so maybe it's not all that serious."

"That's good news, I guess," she said and walked out of the room, Brett trailing behind her as she returned to the living room and plopped back onto the couch.

"We do have some good news," he said and explained the link he had discovered between Ramirez and Kennedy, as well as the possibility that they would soon have an ID for the cop who might be leaking information.

"That is definitely good news. I might just be able to sleep tonight," she said with a smile.

A half grin crept across Brett's full lips. A boyish grin that drove away the earlier sadness she had seen from his eyes.

"You were doing a pretty good job of sawing logs not that

long ago," he teased, and the grin erupted into a full-fledged smile.

She wagged a finger back and forth in a shaming gesture. "You were a pretty good lumberjack yourself."

He jammed his hands on his hips, let out a whoop of a laugh, but then turned serious as Mango popped to her feet, faced the deck and growled.

Brett rushed toward the door and gestured for Anita to move behind him. As he walked toward the door, hand on his weapon, he turned and said to her, "Don't move from there."

With a hand gesture to Mango, he said, "*K noze*, Mango. *K noze*."

The dog instantly hugged Brett's side.

BRETT WENT TO the back door and peered through the glass.

A shadow on the dock. Moving slowly along the length of the boat.

There was little moonlight so Brett couldn't see his face until the person stepped toward the bow of the boat. A light on the deck shined on the man's face and Brett thought he recognized him as one of Jake's neighbors.

He opened the back door and stepped onto the deck, Mango plastered to his side.

"Is that you, Jim?" he called out, but never moved his hand away from his weapon.

"Brett?" the man responded and smiled. "I didn't know you were down. I was checking things out since I thought I saw someone here and knew Jake was away."

Brett relaxed and signaled Mango to lie down. After the dog had complied, Brett stepped down to the walkway to shake the man's hand. "Good to see you again, Jim."

"Same, Brett," he said and motioned to the boat. "She's a beauty, isn't she?"

"She is. My dad has been wishing for one for years. Jake

is a lucky man," he said and ran a hand across the metal railing on the boat.

"I'll say. Imagine winning a cool million in the lottery," Jim said with a low whistle as he admired the boat.

"Wow, a million, huh?" he said, his gut twisting as he realized his friend had lied to him and possibly to his neighbor.

Jim nodded and smiled, but the smile dimmed as his gaze skipped down to the gun at Brett's hip and then back up to his face.

"Trouble?" Jim asked.

He remembered then that the neighbor was a retired police officer, which might work in his favor.

"Just came straight from work. I'm a K-9 agent for SBS in Miami," he said.

Jim's eagle-eyed officer's gaze skipped to Mango lying nearby. "Your partner, I assume."

With a dip of his head, Brett said, "Her name is Mango. She's a good partner."

"Good to hear. Well, it's late and now that I know everything's okay here, I'll go," Jim said.

As the man turned to walk back to his home, Brett said, "Thanks for keeping an eye on things for Jake. If you see anything out of line around here—"

"I'll let you know. Stay safe," Jim said and glanced back toward Jake's house, where Anita's silhouette was visible by the back door.

"Thanks, Jim." He waited on the dock until Jim had gone into his own home to click his tongue for Mango to follow him back into Jake's house.

"You know him?" Anita asked as he entered the living room.

Nodding, he said, "Jake's neighbor Jim. Retired cop who saw something here and decided to check it out. We're lucky to have cop's eyes next door."

"Cop's eyes? Is that a thing?" she asked and sat back down on the couch.

"Yeah, it is. They don't miss a thing. That's why he was out there, inspecting," he said, but then quickly blurted out, "Jim said Jake told him he won the lottery and that's how he bought the boat."

She sat silently for a long moment but plucked at the hem of her shorts nervously. "But Jake told you something different," she finally said.

"He did, and who knows what the truth really is," Brett said and wiped his face with his hands, his beard rasping with the action.

BRETT WAS CLEARLY troubled by his friend's lies, his gaze dark and filled with worry.

"Maybe there's nothing there. Maybe he just doesn't want people to know his business," Anita said, trying to make him feel better.

"Maybe. Hopefully Trey will be able to find out more," he said, then crossed his arms against his chest and rocked back and forth on his heels. "It's late. You should think about sawing some more logs," he said, obviously trying to lighten the mood.

She jumped to her feet and smoothed the fleece of the shorts with her hands. "I should. We have a big day tomorrow."

"Big day?" he asked, puzzled.

She laughed and tapped his flat midsection. "Shopping, big boy. Or did you forget what you said earlier?"

A chuckle burst from him, and he shook his head. "I remember. Get some sleep."

She walked over, rose on her tiptoes and kissed him. Just a quick, butterfly-light peck. And then another.

It just seemed so natural, so familiar as she leaned into him, and he wrapped an arm around her waist to hold her close.

Dug his hand into her hair and undid the topknot she wore, letting her hair spill down.

He tangled his fingers in the strands and he almost groaned. "I always loved the feel of your hair in my hands. The smell of it. You still smell the same."

"You…do…too," she said in between kisses, savoring the masculine scent that had never left her brain. A fresh and citrusy cologne. Brett, all musky and male.

His aroma and the feel of his hard body, even harder now, tangled around her, urging her even closer. Calling her to rub her hips along his, against the obvious proof of his desire.

He groaned and cupped the back of her head, deepening his kiss. Dancing his tongue in to taste her before his body shook and he tempered the kisses and reluctantly shifted away.

"I want you, Anita. I can't deny that," he said and leaned his forehead against hers so that their gazes were eye level. "I've missed you forever, but now—"

"Isn't the right time for this. You've said that before," she reminded, and stepped away from him, arms wrapped around herself to keep it together.

She whirled on him, frustration and need fueling her anger. "I get it. You have responsibilities. You have to keep me safe, and I have a business to think about. One that consumes my entire life."

"You know that's right," he said, hands held out in pleading.

With an angry slash of her hand, she said, "Enough. I get it. But what if tonight is all the time we have left?"

She didn't wait for his reply. She bolted and raced to her bedroom, slammed the door shut. The loud thud of the door as it closed was somehow satisfying.

But the silence that followed…

She'd been alone for so long. Alone except for her business and chefs. The few men she'd given entry into her life had drifted in and out of it because she'd been too busy at work.

Too busy to have a life, but if she was honest with herself, staying busy had kept her from having time to think about the loneliness. To think about the one man whom she had never forgotten.

And now here he was because of the most unlikely of reasons.

Because someone was trying to kill her.

A frisson of fear skittered down her spine and drove away the anger, fear and need.

She wrapped her arms around herself and walked to the window. The night was still. Nothing moved outside except an occasional bubble and ripple in the waters of the canal. Fish, probably, she told herself.

Mango's growl sounded in the other room, causing Anita to pull back slightly from the window. A second later an odd-shaped silhouette came into view, and as the moonlight shone on it, she realized what it was.

A large green-and-fluorescent-orange iguana inched across the railing of the deck. With its long black-and-yellowish-banded tail, it had to be at least five feet long.

No threat. Not this time, anyway.

Luckily Mango was alert. Brett was lucky to have her. Anita was lucky to have both of them guarding her.

With that thought in mind, she told herself not to make Brett's life even harder than it was.

She'd stay away from him as he requested. For now. Maybe even for after.

He'd hurt her once before and she'd be a fool to let it happen again.

BRETT PACED BACK and forth across the narrow width of the living room, too awake after all that had happened.

Jim on the dock. The iguana.

Brett appreciated how alert Mango could be. It lifted a huge weight off his shoulders to know he had a second set of ears to help keep Anita safe.

Keeping Anita safe was the number one priority, which meant he had to stay focused.

He couldn't let their past relationship and lingering emotions take his focus off what was important.

With that in mind, he whipped out his phone to see if he had any text or email messages.

No texts but he had an email from Sophie forwarding the cleaned-up version of the photo he'd found online as well as other images that had been captured from the police station's CCTV footage.

The enhancement of the online photo confirmed that it was Ramirez and Santiago. And neither of the two men seemed happy.

If Santiago was one of Hollywood's goons and Ramirez owed the mobster money, it could explain what had happened the other night.

Which brought even greater worry. Would Hollywood keep on coming for Anita even if Santiago was caught?

He ran through all the permutations in his brain and decided Hollywood wouldn't come after Anita. It was way more likely he'd take out Santiago and his accomplice to avoid them spilling their guts to the police.

Unless Santiago and his accomplice got to Anita first. That was the real threat.

Opening the second email, he flipped through the images, scrutinizing them carefully to see if there was anything familiar about the officer. The man had hidden well, face always averted as he did Hollywood's dirty work.

Muttering a curse beneath his breath, he sat back down at the table and opened his laptop, but then shut it down. It was hours past midnight and even though he could function on only a few hours of sleep, he needed to get some rest to be alert.

The bed would be way more comfortable, but it was just too close to Anita.

And the two easiest entryways were visible from the living room and couch.

For safety's sake, he signaled Mango, walked her toward the front door and instructed her to guard the area. *"Pozor,"* he said and repeated it although the dog had so far proved to understand the command quite well.

Mango peered up at him and seemed to nod before splaying across the front door, head on her paws.

Satisfied, he returned to the living room and was about to sit when the need to see Anita was safe called him.

He walked to her door, leaned his ear close and listened. That soft snore confirmed she was asleep.

Opening the door a crack, he peered inside, worried about someone accessing the window.

All was good and he had no doubt that if Jake's neighbor Jim noticed anything, since Anita's bedroom was closest to the dock and Jim's home, he'd take action.

Satisfied that he could stand down for a few hours of sleep, he grabbed a pillow and blanket from his bedroom and settled in on the couch. Slipping his holster from his belt, he removed the gun and placed it within easy reach on the coffee table.

But as he lay there, a maelstrom of thoughts and images spun around his brain, making for an uneasy sleep.

His eyes had barely drifted shut when he noticed the lightening of the morning sky through the window. It bathed the room in shades of rosy gray and pale lavender.

A quick glance at his phone warned it was nearly seven. No new messages or texts. Regardless it was time to get up and get moving.

Shower first, he thought, rubbing his face and hair with his hand.

Mango was guarding the door, but she'd need to be walked

soon. A quick peek into Anita's room confirmed she was still asleep, and he closed the door to avoid waking her.

Snagging a fresh shirt and underwear from his room, he showered and dressed in fresh clothes and his one pair of jeans. Hopefully he could buy another pair or two today.

Anita still hadn't stirred so he leashed Mango and walked her in the front yard and then did a loop around the house, making sure all was in order.

Nothing had changed since the night before, although he did notice the curtains on Jim's house shift as he walked along the dock. The old cop keeping watch.

When he returned to the house, the strong and welcoming smell of bacon filled the small space as he opened the door.

Anita. Cooking. The kitchen had always been her refuge and that hadn't changed.

But so much else had. Maybe too much.

Armed with that reality, he pushed into the kitchen.

Chapter Fifteen

She didn't register the footsteps until she sensed a presence behind her.

Granny fork raised like a weapon, heart hammering in her chest, she whirled, ready to defend herself.

"Brett. You scared the life out of me," she said and laid a hand on her chest to calm her racing heart.

"I'm sorry. I thought you heard Mango and me come in," he said and took a step back, hands raised as he gave her some space to recover.

She waved off his apology. "No, I'm sorry. Sometimes I get lost in my head when I'm cooking."

"It's why you're so good at what you do," he said with a smile and an appreciative dip of his head.

"Thanks. Breakfast will be ready soon. Coffee is already made," she said and tilted her head in the direction of the espresso pot.

"Can I get you some?" he asked as he walked over.

"No, thanks. I've already had a cup," she said, which was maybe why she was as jittery as she was.

She shouldn't have been that surprised when Brett had returned. She'd seen him walking Mango past her window when she'd woken and knew he wouldn't leave her alone.

She blamed the jitters on the coffee as she grabbed the bagel from the toaster and split it between the two plates she'd warmed in the oven. A little Mornay sauce she'd made from the remains of a bar of cream cheese, butter and Swiss cheese slices went next. She topped the sauce with slices of crispy bacon and a little more cheese sauce.

Returning to the stove, she cracked the last two eggs from the fridge into the bacon grease and fried them, making sure the whites were tight, but the yolks stayed runny. Satisfied they were exactly right, she topped each of the towers of bagel, cheese sauce and bacon with a fried egg. She finished the dish with some salt and pepper.

"Wow. That looks and smells delicious," Brett said as she placed the plate in front of him.

"A fridge cleaner. There wasn't much in there and we've run through most of what we brought with us since we didn't take much," she said with a shrug, hoping the dish would satisfy a big man like Brett.

Brett broke into the egg and the yolk drizzled down, melding with the cheese sauce. He forked up a healthy portion, ate it and hummed in appreciation. "This is amazing. Really amazing," he said and dug into the meal.

His enjoyment of her food drove away the last of her jitters as well as misgivings about what had been a slapdash dish concocted from a hodgepodge of ingredients.

It awakened her own appetite, and she ate, pleased with the final product. "I could probably make you a real croque madame if we're able to do some shopping today."

He nodded. "I just want to check with the team. If they give the go-ahead, you can call your sous-chef and parents, and after we'll get supplies."

"Thanks for remembering about the call," she said, grateful for his understanding.

THERE WAS NOTHING he didn't remember about her, he thought, but didn't say.

"Let me clean up—"

She held her hand up to stop him. "I'll do it so you can make the call. Do anything else you have to."

"Roger that," he said and pushed away from the table, coffee cup in hand.

He dialed Trey and it rang a few times, which was unlike his friend. When he finally answered, he was out of breath, as if he'd been running.

"Sorry, but things are a little off the wall here this morning. Roni's in labor," Trey said.

"She's okay, right? Isn't it early?" he asked, worried since Trey had said she wasn't feeling well the night before.

"It's about a month early, but so far so good. Mia is taking over for me and can fill you in on what we've got so far," Trey said, barely audible over the noises in the background. Someone exhorting someone to breathe. A pained groan.

"Have to go," Trey said and ended the call.

"Is there a problem?" Anita asked and walked over, drying her hands on a kitchen towel.

"Roni's in labor. I have to call Mia for an update," he said and immediately dialed her number, then put the phone on speaker.

"*Buenos dias*, Brett," Mia said as she answered.

"Is it a good day, Mia?" he responded.

"It is. We've been able to identify the leak at the police station, but he's lawyered up," Mia advised.

"Wouldn't you? He's on the hook for those cops who were shot in Aventura," he said.

"Maybe more than that," Mia said with sigh.

"What do you mean?" Anita asked, obviously not liking what she was hearing.

He wasn't liking it, either, especially as Mia said, "Jogger saw a gator chomping on something this morning. Called the cops, who discovered the gator had an arm with a cast in its mouth."

"I'm not getting the connection to the case," Brett said, puzzled by this new development.

"When the coroner cut off the cast, he noticed there were some pretty serious bite marks, damage to the forearm muscles and a small fracture," Mia advised.

It all came together for Brett. "Damage like that which would occur if a pit bull was really holding on and shaking the man's arm. You think this is one of the people who attacked us in Homestead."

"I do and so does the coroner. He'd heard about the attack and put two and two together when he saw the injuries. He's taking DNA from the arm, but he's also taking DNA from the wound to confirm what kind of dog did the biting. If the victim has a record, we'll get a match on the DNA, and also from his fingerprints."

"Someone is tying up loose ends," Anita said in a small voice, clearly fearing she'd be next.

"He is, but we've plugged that leak. You're safe where you are," Mia said to calm her.

"But the cop isn't talking," Anita said, her confusion apparent.

"He isn't but once he hears there's a murder involved, he may want a plea deal, right?" Brett asked.

"Right. We've already reached out to our uncle in the DA's office to see how they can help get more info out of that cop with a plea deal," Mia confirmed.

"Are we safe enough for Anita to call her sous-chef and for us to get some supplies? We're running a little low," Brett said and glanced at Anita. Hopefulness filled her face, and as Mia acknowledged that it was clear for them to do that, a small smile slipped onto her features.

"Great. Keep us posted," he said.

Brett swiped to end the call and handed the phone to Anita. "Once you make this call, I'll burn this phone."

ANITA TOOK THE phone with shaky hands, almost dreading what she might hear from Melanie.

Her sous-chef answered on the first ring. "Anita?" she asked, a puzzled tone in her voice since she likely didn't recognize the number.

"Yes, it's me. I can't use my own phone. How are things?" she asked and braced herself for bad news.

"We miss you, but you trained us well. We got the steaks delivered as promised along with some extra filets to make up for it. We're all set for the next few days with the menu you left for us," Melanie advised, her voice relaxed, almost bordering on cheery.

But is it forced cheeriness?

"Are you sure, Melanie? I shouldn't be worried?" Anita urged, cell phone pressed so hard to her ear that her diamond stud dug into her flesh.

"I'm sure, Anita. Like I said, you trained us to handle things. Take care of things so you can come back quickly," Melanie said as someone called out to her.

"Chef, we need you here," one of her line chefs said.

"Don't worry, Chef," Melanie repeated and then the line went dead.

She dialed her parents next and it instantly went to voice mail. They had likely ignored the unfamiliar number. She left a detailed message and tried her best to tell them not to worry and that she was safe.

She handed the phone back to Brett, almost distractedly.

"It's all good, right?" he asked, ducking down so that he could read her face more clearly.

"It's all good," she repeated and actually believed it. Meeting his gaze, she said, "How about we do that shopping now."

TONY HOLLYWOOD'S FACE was buried in his hands, elbows braced on his desk, as Santiago limped into his office.

"What's up, boss?" he asked.

As Tony straightened, he could swear he saw the remnants of tears on his face and even though he knew the likely reason for it, he played stupid.

"Something wrong?"

"My sister called. The cops called to say Billy's dead. They found his arm—his freakin' arm—in a gator," Tony said and slammed his hands on the surface of the desk.

The sound was as loud as a gunshot, making him jump.

"I'm sorry, boss. What happened?" he said, feigning ignorance.

With speed he didn't think possible for a man of Tony's size, Tony rounded the corner, grabbed his throat and propelled him against the wall. He tightened his hold and lifted him off the ground, choking him.

"What happened to Billy?" Tony asked, nose to nose with him now that he had him half a foot in the air.

"Don't...know," he managed to squeak out with the little air he could breathe.

Tony tossed him away like a rag doll and, thanks to his injured leg, he crumpled to the ground.

Tony paced back and forth, raking a hand through his hair, muttering over and over as he did so. "He was family. My sister's heart is broken. He was her only child."

"I didn't do it," he lied, fearing that he'd underestimated Tony's love for his incompetent nephew.

Tony spun and cursed him out, veins bulging on his neck and forehead, angry red blossoming on his face.

"Liar. I should have you offed. You're nothing but a liability," he said with a toss of a hand in his direction.

"You should but you won't because you know I have insurance, don't you?" he said, pulling the ace card he had tucked up his sleeve.

Tony clenched his fists and shuffled his feet, almost like a bull getting ready to charge, but then he stopped and stepped back.

"Get out of here. Find the girl. Finish her off," he said from behind gritted teeth.

Santiago eased his hands into his pockets, turned and sashayed away, a newfound sense of power flowing through his veins. But he couldn't be overconfident.

He'd misjudged Tony's reaction to Billy's death, but he hoped that in time Tony would realize that he'd done the right thing. Billy had been nothing but a liability. The weakest link in the chain leading to him and eventually to Tony.

Yeah, Tony would thank him one day, he thought, and headed out to his car.

Anita Reyes and the SBS K-9 agent had flown the coop, but his mole at the police station had been very helpful so far. He had hoped to end the problem in Aventura, but the SBS agents had been too quick thinking. And Billy and that damn dog had totally messed things up in Homestead.

He should have handled it by himself and from now on he would.

First step: see what his mole could tell him.

Chapter Sixteen

Brett hauled the half-a-dozen bags onto the kitchen counter. They landed with a resounding and very pleasing thunk. Anita followed him in carrying the packages with their new clothing, Mango at her side. She passed by the kitchen, probably to take the bags to their bedrooms, and Mango tagged along with her, carrying a small bag.

All the purchases were courtesy of the cash in the pouch Trey had instructed him to take from the desk drawer. Cash was king to avoid anyone tracking his credit card.

But to do that they had to know who he was, and it worried him that the mole at the police force might have overheard his name and shared it with Santiago and his cronies. Luckily, he'd never been one to overly share on social media.

But can you say the same for your friends? he thought as he unpacked the bags onto the counter.

That was especially worrisome considering Jake and the changing stories about the cash for the boat.

Not that he'd let on about those fears to Anita.

For the first time in the last two days, the worry had seemed to slip from her as they'd shopped. He hadn't wanted to bring her down by sharing his concerns.

She almost skipped back into the kitchen to help him unpack. Mango walked beside her but left her to drink some fresh water Brett had set out that morning.

"I put the bag with your things on your bed," she said.

"Thanks. Do you mind finishing up so I can check in with Mia and Trey?" he said and wiggled a burner phone in the air in emphasis.

"Go ahead. I can handle this."

He signaled Mango to guard the door and walked to his bedroom, wanting some privacy for the call.

Trey didn't answer and his gut knotted with fear.

It had been a few hours since they'd spoken. But labor could take that long, he told himself and dialed Mia.

She answered on the first ring. "How's Roni?" he asked, his best friend's very pregnant wife first and foremost in his mind.

"Still in labor. I spoke to Trey about an hour ago and everything seems to be going well," she said.

"That's good news. Any new developments?" he asked.

"Our suspect cop still isn't talking, but his lawyer is negotiating with my uncle on a plea deal. I'm no legal expert, but if it avoids having the felony murder rule apply, I think he'd be wise to take it," Mia replied, confidence ringing in her voice.

"Is it too soon for the DNA results on the gator victim?" he asked, aware that it sometimes took days or weeks depending on resources and backlogs.

"The coroner has a new rapid DNA test, but he's double-checking the results," she said, some of her earlier confidence fading.

He narrowed his gaze as he considered what might be wrong and said, "Is there a problem? Contamination maybe?"

A long pause and awkward cough was followed by, "Possibly. Police have an ID on the gator victim from the fingerprints. It's William Allen. Tony's nephew."

"Wow. Do you think Hollywood killed his own nephew?" he asked, shocked and yet not shocked. Ruthless mobsters like Hollywood had rubbed out family on more than one occasion.

"It gets more complicated than that. The blood from the

suspect you shot and that from the gator victim show a familial connection," she explained.

"But the second Homestead attacker was probably Kennedy," Brett said and as his mind processed the new info, he added, "We have nothing that says he's related to Hollywood."

"You're right. If the second set of tests come back the same, we'll have to dig deeper into how that's possible," Mia said.

The sound of Anita putting things away in the kitchen ended. Her soft footfalls coming down the hall warned of her imminent arrival.

Since he didn't want to worry her, maybe it was time to wind down this conversation. But before he did so, he had one last question to ask.

"Have you been able to find out anything more about Jake and the boat?"

THE PHONE RANG and rang before going to voice mail.

It was the third time he'd tried to call his mole, but the third time hadn't been a charm.

His intuition warned that it wasn't a good thing that his cop wasn't answering.

He'd been compromised, which meant he wouldn't be getting more information from him.

But he wasn't the only mark tangled up with Hollywood. Santiago just had to pull the right strings to find someone who could give him the info he needed to find the chef and the SBS agent.

BRETT STOOD IN the middle of the room, head bent dejectedly. He scraped his hand across his short-cropped hair and said, "Yeah, I get it. I appreciate you working on that."

He ended the call and faced her with a forced smile. "No news on Roni. She's still in labor."

"What about the investigation? Anything?" she pressed.

"Cop still isn't talking, but Mia is confident they'll be able to work out a plea deal for his cooperation. They're double-checking the analysis. As for Jake, Trey and Mia's aunt, who's some hotshot lawyer, searched but couldn't find any evidence of Jake filing a Lejeune claim," he said. Every inch of his body communicated that not all was well with the case.

His upset transferred itself to her and she wrapped her arms around herself, trying to rein in fear and stay calm.

"What do we do now?" she asked.

"We keep on digging," he said and gestured toward the window in the room and the dock outside. "We start with that boat. Jake had to register it, and to do that he had to prove ownership. If we can find out who sold it to him, maybe they can tell us more about how he paid for it."

"You're still that worried about Jake?" she asked, trying to understand why he wouldn't trust an old friend, until she remembered.

"You're afraid to trust him because of what happened in Iraq," she said, then walked up to him and cradled his cheek. "It's okay to trust your friend."

He shook his head hard, dislodging her hand, and tapped his index finger against his chest. "Not when there are conflicting stories about how he bought a quarter-of-a-million-dollar boat. He told me it was a Lejeune settlement. Jim said it was a lottery win. The only likely reason to lie is because it's dirty money."

She couldn't argue with him about that. People lied when they had something to hide.

Nodding, she said, "Agreed. Where do we start?"

HER WORDS, her trust in him, relieved some of the concern that had twisted his gut into a knot during his conversation with Mia.

"We look up the address for the local DMV. They would

have to issue the boat registration," he said, then slipped his hand into hers and gently urged her from the room and back out to the breakfast bar and his laptop.

Mango raised her head and peered at them as they entered, but otherwise didn't shift from her spot guarding the door.

It took only a few minutes to get an address, and armed with that and Mango, whom he leashed to take with them, they went outside so he could find the boat registration. He lowered the lift until the boat was low enough that he could climb aboard.

"Wait here," he said and handed Mango's leash to Anita.

He hopped on and immediately noticed the glove box in the boat's console. He popped it open and pulled out a plastic envelope that held an owner's manual and the boat registration. He examined the owner's manual, hoping that it might have the seller's name on it, but no luck. Same with the boat registration, which only had Jake's name on it.

Shoving the materials back into the envelope, he took them with him as he got off the boat. He slipped his hand into Anita's and signaled Mango to heel.

"Time to hit the DMV."

SANTIAGO HAD PULLED on more strings than he thought possible.

None had turned up any information that could lead him to where the chef and SBS agent might have gone.

Frustrated, he banged his palm on the steering wheel and wracked his brains for any other names, running through them until one suddenly came to him.

It would be a big ask and he might have to sacrifice the money owed to Hollywood to get the info, but it would be worth it.

Pulling a burner phone from his jacket pocket, he made the call.

LUCKILY, THE DMV office on the Overseas Highway was a short five-minute ride from Jake's house since there was barely an hour left before it closed. It was in a strip mall that held a large supermarket, clothing outlet, public library and an assortment of other stores.

At the late hour, there was little activity inside the DMV and a young woman at a window quickly flagged them to come over.

Brett turned on the charm since honey always caught more flies than vinegar.

"I was hoping you could help us out. My friend Jake Winston—"

"I know Jake well," she said, which came as no surprise to Brett.

The young woman—pretty, blonde and athletic from what was visible through the window—was totally Jake's type. Plus, the locals were a close-knit group from what he had seen in past visits with his friend.

"Jake and I were in the Marines together and I was hoping you could help me out with something," he said and gave her his most boyish grin.

"Like what?" she asked, puzzlement on her features.

Placing the boat registration in the window slot, he tapped it and said, "Would you have helped Jake register this boat?"

Her gaze narrowed, shifted from him to Anita and then to Mango. "Is that a service dog?" she asked, her earlier friendliness dimming.

"Mango's my partner. I work with SBS. I'm not a cop, if that's what you're worried about. Jake is my best friend. I want to surprise him with something new for his boat," he said, and to prove it, he turned his left wrist over and shifted his watch so she could see the tattoo of the bulldog that he and all of his unit had gotten one drunken night.

The woman leaned forward, which gave him a clear view of her generous chest, but then she plopped back onto her high stool and smiled. "I helped Jake with the paperwork. He got the boat not far from here. Bob's Shipyard."

"Thanks. That's all I needed. I'll be sure to let Jake know you helped us," he said and gave her a little salute in thanks.

As they walked away from the window, Anita muttered under her breath, "Boy, can you turn on the charm."

He laughed and glanced in her direction. "You should know," he teased.

She stopped dead then and faced him, her gaze skipping all across his face. Pointing toward the DMV office, she said, "It was never fake with us the way it was in there."

He grew more serious and dipped his head in agreement. "It was never fake with you. Never," he said, cupped her cheek and leaned down to kiss her.

Chapter Seventeen

It was a kiss of promise and maybe possibly forgiveness for all that had gone wrong between them.

When he broke the kiss, he grinned, and it caused her heart to do a little flip-flop. She still wasn't immune to his charm. His real charm and not the act he had put on for Jake's fangirl in the DMV office.

Together, Mango comfortably at her side, they returned to their car. Brett harnessed Mango into the back seat, and once they were settled, Brett programmed the car for the ride to the boat dealer.

Bob's Shipyard was over half an hour away in Islamorada. As they passed multiple boat sale stores along the way, she said, "I wonder why he went that far to buy the boat."

Brett shrugged and it was clear he'd been wondering the same thing himself. "Maybe they were the only ones with the model he wanted."

"Or maybe Bob's Shipyard was the only place that wouldn't ask questions about how Jake was paying for it," she said.

Brett's lips tightened into a grimace, but he reluctantly nodded. "That's a very real possibility."

"But you don't want to believe there's anything criminal about how Jake got the money?" she pressed.

He bobbed his head, the movement stilted. Harsh. "I don't want to believe but it worries me. Jake didn't file a Lejeune settlement claim."

"Which leaves the lottery explanation," Anita said as Brett drove past yet another shipyard advertising boats for sale.

"Jake bought the boat a month ago. Florida keeps lottery winner names private for three months," Brett said, hands tight on the wheel.

She processed that info, trying to understand why Jake would lie about a settlement rather than tell Brett about the lottery win.

Brett must have been thinking the same thing since a second later he said, "Maybe he was worried I was going to hit him up for a loan. Some of our unit members have had a rough time. A couple are even homeless. Jake and I try to help when we can, but maybe he was worried people would come out of the woodwork once they found out about the lottery win."

"But he told Jim about it," Anita pushed.

Another shrug, followed by, "He didn't see Jim that way. As a taker."

She bit back that it meant Jake saw him as a taker because she didn't want to hurt him any more than he must be hurting.

Brett's comment created a pall in the vehicle that even Mango sensed since she sat up and whined.

Anita reached back and petted the pit bull, reassuring her that all was well. Mango licked her hand, dragging a laugh from her.

"Mango likes you," Brett said, watching the interaction in the rearview mirror.

"I'm glad," she said and rubbed the dog's ears and head again, earning another doggy kiss.

A ghost of a smile drifted across his lips. "I'm glad, too," he said and slowed the car.

She looked out the window and noticed the sign for Bob's Shipyard. Hopefully Brett would get the answers that confirmed his trust in his friend hadn't been misplaced.

Santiago cursed as yet another online search came up blank for the SBS agent.

Brett Madison was the name that his contact at the FBI had provided.

Whoever he was, he had done an excellent job of scrubbing himself off the internet.

Either that or the SBS team had done it for him.

He pulled up the agency's website again and stared at the smiling faces of the Gonzalez family members who ran it.

Much like what had happened with Madison, there was little private info for the family members, except for Mia Gonzalez, now Mia Gonzalez Wilson.

Mia and her cousin Carolina had been top influencers before Mia had cut back on those activities to join her family's agency and marry John Wilson, a wealthy tech CEO.

There were hundreds of thousands of hits for Mia thanks to the successful business her cousin and she had run. He started reviewing them, but after scrolling through dozens of pages, he gave up on that angle because there were just too many articles, and most were about public events.

He went back to the website for the agency and tried to find out more about the acting head, Ramon Gonzalez III who was sometimes referred to as "Trey." Probably because he was the third Ramon.

Much as with the elusive Brett Madison, there was little confidential information online. But since Trey had been a detective on several high-profile cases, there were news articles galore. The only thing he could glean from them was Gonzalez's age and that he'd once been a marine.

Santiago closed his eyes, trying to remember what had happened in Homestead.

The dog attack on Billy.

Poor Billy, he thought for a fleeting moment.

The man commanding the dog in some foreign language.

A big man. Tall and broad-shouldered. Thickly muscled and hard-bodied and yet he had moved quickly. Decisively.

The way a soldier might.

That sent him down another rabbit hole, trying to locate any stories that might tie Gonzalez and Madison.

Well over an hour passed with nothing and his stomach grumbled, complaining that it was dinnertime.

He picked up his cell phone and ordered a Cubano, mango *batido* and *maduros* from a local place that had the best Cuban sandwiches and shakes.

Handheld food because he didn't intend to leave that computer until he had a clue as to where he would find the elusive Brett Madison and the chef who could send him to the electric chair.

THE NEWS CAME as they were driving back from the boat dealer.

After many long hours of labor, Roni had given birth to a baby girl they'd named Marielena after the two families' grandmothers.

"Roni and the baby are both doing well," Trey said.

Brett didn't miss the fatigue in his friend's voice. "How are you doing?"

"Exhausted," Trey admitted, but then quickly tacked on, "But I'm headed to the office now that I know Roni and the baby are fine."

He shared a look with Anita, who seemed to be totally in sync with him. "Maybe you should stay with Roni and your new daughter."

"Roni understands. Believe me. She's already been on the phone with her partner," Trey said.

Brett hated to ask, but Trey had opened the door with his statement.

"Any news on the cop or the plea deal?"

"Williams told Roni that the plea deal was in place. Williams is in the interview room with him right now. As soon as I know more, I'll let you know," Trey said as the sound of voices nearby faded into silence when he apparently stepped out of the hospital.

"I have something to share as well. You may be able to take Jake off your plate. Jake's neighbor and the dealer he bought the boat from told us Jake won a big lottery prize a month ago. That's how he got the cash for the boat."

"We'll try to confirm that, but it seems like your gut wasn't wrong about going to Jake's," Trey replied, the subtext clear.

"I'm glad, too. We'll talk to you later," he said.

"Video call twenty-two hundred. Maybe we'll have more news by then."

"Roger," Brett said and ended the call.

"SEEMS LIKE GOOD news all around," Anita said, trying to understand why Brett didn't seem more excited about all the progress and his friend's happy event.

An abrupt nod was her only answer.

Brett did a quick glance at the cell phone. "It's well past dinnertime. I don't know about you, but I'm hungry."

In response her stomach did a little growl, dragging a chuckle from her. "I'm a mite peckish," she joked and covered her noisy belly with a hand.

"I think we can risk dinner out since things seem under control for now," he said and executed a quick U-turn back toward Islamorada.

Barely five minutes later they were at a local restaurant that Anita recognized as an icon in the Keys. It had been around since the 1940s and was famous for its turtle chowder, classic Keys food and down-home dishes.

"I've heard about this place, but I've never been here," she said and shot a quick look back at Mango. "Will we able to bring Mango in?"

Brett tracked her gaze and shook his head. "I'm not sure, but probably not. Would you mind takeout and a picnic? It might be more secure to not let a lot of people see us as well."

"I'm game. Let's check out the menu online," she said, and within a few minutes they'd placed an order for conch fritters, turtle chowder and fresh-caught grilled wahoo and snapper. For Mango they added meat loaf with mashed potatoes, apparently a favorite of the pit bull.

They parked in front of the restaurant's patio with the colorful sea turtles where diners could wait for a table. Barely twenty minutes later, a server approached with a large shopping bag.

Brett stepped out to grab their order and slipped the bag into the back seat by Mango. Easing into the driver's seat again, he pulled out of the parking lot and turned onto the Old Highway. A few blocks up, another turn had them driving through a neighborhood of cinder block ranch homes on postage-stamp lots dotted with palm trees, crotons and other tropical plants and flowers.

They hadn't gone far when they reached a cul-de-sac with parking next to a beach access point.

Anita stepped out of the car and took hold of the bag with their food while Brett grabbed a blanket from the back of the car, unharnessed Mango and leashed her for the walk onto the beach. But as he did so, he peered around, clearly still vigilant despite his earlier comment that everything seemed to be under control for the moment.

"We're good to go," he said and together they walked down a path between some beachside houses and to the sand until they were several yards from the water, where Brett spread out the blanket for them to sit.

Once they were comfortably settled, Mango stretched out beside Brett on the blanket, they emptied the bag and spread the take-out dishes between them. Finding the conch fritters, they shared those first, laughing and talking as they ate.

It was easy for her mind and heart to drift back to when they used to date and how wonderful it had been between them. But every now and then, Brett would scan the area around them, reminding her that this wasn't just like it once was.

Someone was still trying to kill her, and it was only a matter of time before the peace they were feeling now would be shattered.

It dimmed her appetite, enough that Brett noticed she had stopped eating what was an absolutely wonderful grilled wahoo and started picking at it.

He offered her a smile and cradled her cheek. "It's going to be okay, Anita. Trust me."

She dropped her plastic fork onto her plate, shook her head and said, "Trust you? Seriously?"

His face hardened, confirming her shot had struck home on so many levels.

How could she trust a man who had ghosted her, but worse, trust a man who didn't trust himself?

She waited for an explosion of anger, almost welcoming it if it would clear the air around them.

But Brett only stared straight ahead, his body ramrod stiff, muscles tense. Hands taut on the plastic take-out tray with his meal.

In clipped tones, he said, "Yes, trust me. I would do anything to keep you safe."

As he finished, he slowly faced her, eyes blazing with emotion. "Anything, Anita. Don't doubt that."

She muttered a curse and looked away from that intense gaze because deep in her heart she didn't doubt him.

That almost scared her more.

"Don't die for me, Brett. Please don't," she said, aware that he wouldn't hesitate to do that. As both a soldier and SBS agent, Brett had committed to risk his life to protect others. That duty was as much a part of his DNA as the color of his hair and eyes.

Brett slipped an arm around her shoulders and drew her close. "It won't get to that, my love. It won't."

Throat tight with emotion, she said, "Promise me."

With a half smile on his face, he nodded and said, "I promise."

Mango, sensing the emotion and tension, popped away from her plate of food to stand before them, nose slathered with the remnants of meat loaf and mashed potatoes until her tongue swept out to lick them away.

It dragged laughs from them, ending the emotional moment and restoring the peace she had been feeling when they had first sat to eat.

Brett playfully bumped her shoulder with his and tossed Mango a bit of his fish that the dog snagged midair and gulped down in a single bite.

Their picnic finished with them feeding Mango the remnants of their meals. After packing their dishes and cutlery back into the bag, which Brett tossed into a nearby garbage can, they shook out the blanket, folded it and took Mango for a long walk along the beach. The dog needed the activity, but Anita did as well since she wasn't used to just sitting around.

As an executive chef, she spent her days at the market scoping out the freshest ingredients for her restaurant's menu and then on her feet in the kitchen.

She welcomed the walk and the beauty of the beach at night since it had grown dark while they were eating.

A full moon scattered playful light on the surface of the water, making it glitter happily. Lights had snapped on in the homes along the beachfront, casting a warm, welcoming glow on the sand.

The slightest breeze stirred palm trees and the nearby bushes, making them crackle and rustle and prompting Brett to peer in their direction to make sure it was only the breeze and not more.

They reluctantly returned to the car for the trip to Jake's house, aware that Trey had scheduled a meeting for later that night.

The drive back was silent at first, but it was impossible for Anita not to notice that at one point Brett was nervously checking his rearview mirror, on high alert.

As he pulled into the right lane and slowed the car, he glanced at the mirror again and muttered a curse beneath his breath.

"Something wrong?" she asked just to make sure she was reading the signals right.

"Car has been on our tail for about two miles. Windows are too tinted to see who's driving," he said, and with a quick peek at the side mirror, he pulled back into the left lane and raced ahead, so rapidly it pushed her into her seat.

She flipped down the visor and opened the vanity mirror, noted the late model Mercedes sedan that did an exaggerated shift to the left lane, mimicking what Brett had done.

"The shooter at the police station was driving a Mercedes," she said, fear gripping her.

"I know," he said calmly and increased his speed, whipping around a slow-moving car in front of him, so quickly it tossed her from side to side.

He was speeding forward, but Fate intervened as the light just several yards away turned red and an oversize truck jack-rabbited into the intersection.

Brett swore and screeched to a halt to avoid a collision.

The Mercedes that had been tailing them pulled right up next to them at the light.

As the driver's side window on the Mercedes lowered, Brett swept his arm across her body and said, "Get down."

Chapter Eighteen

As soon as Anita hunkered down in the seat, Brett freed his gun from the holster and slid down the passenger side window.

To his surprise, an elderly woman, in her eighties if he had to guess, raised an arthritis-gnarled finger and with a quaver in her voice said, "My husband wants me to let you know your left taillight is broken."

Relief slammed through him, almost violently. He dipped his head, smiled and said, "Thank you, ma'am. I appreciate you letting me know."

Anita must have overheard since she sat up in her seat, her body trembling, a response to the initial adrenaline rush. She wrapped her arms around herself, apparently trying to rein in her fear.

He laid his hand on her shoulder and stroked it back and forth, trying to calm her. "It was just a helpful senior citizen."

Anita scoffed. "Helpful nearly got them shot. I saw you reach for your gun."

He couldn't deny it as he holstered the weapon and someone honked from behind them, annoyed that the light had turned green and they weren't moving.

Driving forward, Brett traveled down the Overseas Highway until they reached the turn for the street that would take them to the almost serpentine labyrinth of roads along the man-made canals where Jake had his home.

He parked in the gravel driveway and raised his hand in

a stop gesture to warn Anita to stay put until he made sure all was safe.

As he freed Mango from the back seat, he noticed a light snap on in the front room of Jim's home. A second later the curtain was drawn slightly away.

Jim checking up on who had arrived.

He waved at the man. The curtain drifted back into place and the light snapped off.

Brett examined the area all around. Quiet along the front of the home.

Walking with Mango to the side door, he let her sniff there for anything out of the ordinary, then walked to the back dock, where everything also seemed in order.

He unlocked the entrance and released Mango to inspect the area. A short while later, Mango returned to the front door and sat, confirming that it was okay for them to enter.

With a hand signal, he commanded Mango to heel, and they returned to the car for Anita.

"All clear," he said and helped her from the car.

Arm around her waist since she still seemed shaken by what had happened earlier, they walked to the side door, where he entered first and confirmed Mango's decision that it was safe. Satisfied, he opened the side door and held out a hand to invite her to come in.

She slipped her hand into his and walked in, but as she did so, she tucked herself against him and said, "Thank you. For everything."

He wanted to say that he was just doing his job, but Anita wasn't just a job. She could never be just that.

Hugging her tight, he bent his head and tucked it to hers, needing that connection. Wishing that they weren't in this situation so that they could rekindle the magic they'd once had, only they weren't those same people anymore.

He was a man with a lot of trust issues and baggage. She was a woman with her own life and a busy one at that.

"I wish…" she whispered against his ear, but stopped, as if knowing what he was thinking and the impossibility of not only the now but also the future.

"I wish, too, but if wishes were horses, beggars would ride," he said, repeating a phrase he'd heard the nuns in his Catholic elementary school utter whenever they'd long for a snow day.

Grudgingly they separated, hopes dashed.

With close to an hour before their big meeting, Anita excused herself to go unpack and wash the clothing they'd bought earlier that day.

He was too wired after the nonincident with the elderly couple, plus pit bulls were typically very active dogs. By now he would have normally walked or exercised Mango a few times, and as good as the dog had been, harnessed into the car or guarding the door, she needed more than the few walks she'd had. Even their earlier walk on the beach probably hadn't been enough.

Because of that, he headed to his bedroom and grabbed the tug toy and hard rubber ball he'd picked up while they'd been shopping.

Anita was at the end of the hall in the small laundry room, and he let her know he was going to exercise Mango.

"I'll meet you in a few minutes," she said.

With little space on the back deck or dock, he went behind his parked car and Jake's boat trailer to the narrow sliver of driveway that remained. There he unleashed Mango and tossed the ball.

The dog took off like a rocket, gravel flying up as she dug her powerful legs into the stone. She snagged the ball as it was still bouncing, whipped around and brought it back to drop it at his feet.

"Good girl," he said and rewarded her with a hearty rub of her squarish head and short pointy ears.

When Anita came out to join them, Mango raced to her and glued herself to her side until Anita bent and stroked her hands all along the pittie's glossy fur and muscular body. "I love you, too," she said, earning a doggy kiss.

Brett handed Anita the ball and for the next half hour or so they played with Mango, having her chase the ball and run through a number of the basic commands. He explained to Anita what each one meant and that he issued the commands in Czech.

"Why Czech?" she asked as he finally instructed the dog to heel so they could return inside for their meeting.

"So the crooks won't know what they mean and so Mango won't react to a commonly used word," he said, and after they entered, he locked up and instructed Mango to guard the back door since he'd have a clean line of sight to the side door from the breakfast bar.

As he had the night before, he powered up his laptop, sent the monitor image to the larger television screen and clicked on the link to join the video meeting.

The SBS crew, except for Roni, were gathered around the table with Roni's partner, Heath Williams, and Mia's husband, John Wilson.

"CONGRATULATIONS TO YOU and Roni, Trey," Anita said.

Deep smudges under his eyes, like swipes of charcoal on a drawing, and thick stubble darkened his otherwise handsome face, but a brilliant smile lit his aqua eyes.

"*Gracias*, Anita. I'm a lucky man. Marielena is a beauty," Trey said and popped up a picture of the new baby, which earned the requisite oohs and aahs from everyone.

"She is at that, Trey. Congrats," Brett said and for a second

Anita thought she detected a wistful note in his tones, but then he was all action.

"I'm hoping for some good news."

Trey and Heath shared a look from across the table and Trey motioned for Heath to report.

"Our crooked cop agreed to a plea deal. He'll still do a good amount of time for the shootings of the two Aventura cops, but he won't get life for Billy Allen's murder," Heath advised.

"Have you found the rest of Billy in the gator?" Brett asked matter-of-factly.

Anita's stomach turned at the thought of what the gator had done to the man and Brett's seemingly uncaring tone. But then again, Billy had tried to kill them and Mango.

Heath nodded and continued. "Homestead police located his remains not far from where the jogger saw the gator with the arm. Coroner says COD was a bullet to the head," Heath said and mimicked a shot to the forehead.

Trey jumped in with, "Same caliber and make as with Ramirez and the stray bullets CSI dug out of the cabinets in Homestead. Ballistics should be able to confirm shortly if all those bullets came from the same gun."

She supposed that was some progress, not that it made her feel any more comfortable with her own situation.

"If I remember correctly, whoever shot Billy might be related to him?" Anita said, recalling something Mia had said the night before.

"Cousins, but what's more interesting is that the shooter is Tony Hollywood's son," Trey replied.

Brett shot a quick look at her, apparently as puzzled as she was since he asked, "Why is it interesting?"

"Because Tony Hollywood's one and only son is currently serving a five-year sentence for aggravated assault," Mia advised.

Anita processed that for a moment and shook her head. "Santiago Kennedy is Tony Hollywood's illegitimate child?"

"And now we have evidence also tying Kennedy to the assault on you in Homestead. Once ballistics confirms whether the bullets are the same, we've got him," Trey said.

"But not Hollywood," Anita said and pushed a stray lock of hair back from her face, feeling frustration despite all the progress that had been made.

Brett wrapped an arm around her shoulders, consoling her with a squeeze. "Once we get Kennedy, he may roll on Hollywood. But even if he doesn't, Hollywood is not going to come after you. There is nothing you know that can hurt Hollywood."

"Brett's right," Trey interjected. "The only person Hollywood should be worried about is Santiago Kennedy. He's the key in all this. He killed Ramirez and I'm sure that he killed Hollywood's nephew."

Everyone around the table nodded in agreement and then John Wilson piped in with, "I ran them through my program and the probability is almost one hundred percent that Kennedy killed both Ramirez and his cousin. But there is also a high probability that we won't get Kennedy alive."

"You think Hollywood is going to kill him?" Anita asked, thinking that the mobster had a lot to worry about with his illegitimate son.

Using his fingers, Wilson counted down the reasons. "One, Kennedy messed up with Ramirez. The program—and my gut—says he wasn't supposed to kill him, just scare him. Two, the nephew's murder. Three, the fear his wife will find out he fooled around. And finally, four, the fear Kennedy will spill his guts as part of a plea deal."

Trey had been nodding along as Wilson spoke and voiced his agreement. "I don't need the program to tell me you're one hundred percent right, John. It's why we have to find Kennedy because he knows Anita is the final nail in the coffin to charging him with Ramirez's murder."

ANITA SHOOK BENEATH his arm at Trey's words.

Brett understood. She was more worried about being in the coffin than being the nail.

He leaned close and whispered in her ear, "We will get him."

She half glanced at him, eyes wide with fear. "But when, Brett. When?"

Her whispered words cut through the air and were picked up by the laptop mic, transmitting them to those seated at the SBS offices.

"Soon. We will have Kennedy soon," Trey promised, earning a chorus of assurances from those gathered around the table.

Buoyed by his colleagues, Brett nevertheless had concerns about one front. "What about the Feds? Still not cooperating?"

"Still not cooperating," Trey said, his annoyance obvious.

Roni's partner, Heath, tacked on, "But we're working on it."

He had to be satisfied with that, Brett supposed. "What are our next steps?"

Trey and Heath glanced at each other from across the table.

"We tie together the ballistics and get a BOLO out for Kennedy. Keep on working on the Feds," Heath said.

"SBS will work on finding out what we can about Kennedy's familial connection to Hollywood. Maybe there's something there that we can use," Trey said.

"Like where he might be hiding?" Anita asked, her body still trembling and tense beneath his arm.

Trey nodded. "Yes, like that. If we find his mother, we may be able to get info from her."

"We can work on that as well," Brett offered, his mind already racing on where he could search for that information.

"How long before they release Allen's body to his family?"

Brett added, thinking that a visit to the funeral mass might also yield valuable insights.

"Not soon. They literally have to piece him together and search all those pieces for evidence. That's going to take time," Heath advised.

"Patience, Brett. I know you feel otherwise, but we've made a lot of progress," Trey shot back, testiness in his tone that made his baby sister, Mia, reach over and lay a hand on his forearm as it rested on the tabletop.

Trey shook his head and looked down, chastised. "As you can imagine, I've had a lot on my mind in the last twenty-four hours."

Although he hadn't said the words, the apology was apparent in his tone and the droop of his head. Brett accepted it and offered his own apology of sorts. "I get it. We've been kind of busy ourselves."

"Luckily, we do have some progress. I think you can rest a little easier tonight," Mia said, stepping in to be the mediator.

"Yes, we can. Maybe it's time we all got some rest," Trey said and rubbed his hands across the stubble on his face.

Brett nodded. "We'll check in tomorrow morning."

"Agreed. Ten hundred sharp," Trey said, and after a quick perusal of the table to see if anyone had anything to add, he ended the call.

"Can we rest easier tonight?" Anita asked, doubt alive in her voice.

Brett understood her concerns and they weren't just about Hollywood and Kennedy. The tension had been building between them for days and the long night loomed large.

He had to do what he could to alleviate her fears and keep from doing something they might both regret.

Chapter Nineteen

Anita swiveled in her seat, wanting to make sure she didn't miss any nuance of Brett's response.

There was the slightest hesitation and furrow of his brow before he said, "We can. It's unlikely Kennedy knows where we are right now and considering what he's done—"

"You mean killing Hollywood's nephew, who is also his cousin?" she jumped in, needing to make sure she understood exactly what was happening.

"For starters. I'd put money on it that Hollywood sent Kennedy to collect a debt, not kill Ramirez. He's probably angry now that he's unlikely to get his money."

"Unless Ramirez's partner knows something he's not talking about. I got the sense that Manny and his partner, Kevin Marino, shared a lot," she said, recalling how close they'd seemed to be the many times she'd interacted with them.

Brett mulled over her comments and nodded. "The police have probably already talked to him, but maybe he'd share more if he wasn't worried about being arrested."

"It's worth investigating, right? That and Kennedy's mother. Who was she? Does Mrs. Hollywood know? I'd be royally pissed if my husband was cheating," she said, then frowned and shook her head. "Not to mention he had a child," she added.

"Any man who cheated on you would need his head examined," he said, a dangerous gleam in his gaze as he fixed it on her and reached up to stroke the back of his hand across her cheek.

"Leaving me isn't much better," she said, then covered his hand with hers and drew it away, but she didn't let go.

He nodded. "I left you. I think I left me as well. I'm not the same man. He's long gone."

Pain colored his words and his body, which sagged from the weight of it.

Squeezing his hand, she tempered her response. "He is, but the man I see here is honorable, brave and loving."

"Does that mean there's hope for us?" he asked, lifting an eyebrow in emphasis.

"Maybe," she said, needing honesty between them.

A smile filled with longing and hopefulness drifted across his lips.

With a final squeeze of his hand, she said, "What do we do now?"

SANTIAGO KEPT TO the shadows in the alley behind Marino's condo building. It had made sense to handle this first before searching for the woman and the SBS agent. If his research was on the money, they were hours away in the Keys.

As a light snapped on a few floors above, he leaped into action, pulling down the ladder for the fire escape and silently climbing until he reached the right condo. His injured leg protested the movement and he limped onto the last landing.

Flattening against the wall, he held his breath until he confirmed he hadn't been seen by Ramirez's partner, Marino, who had just entered the apartment. Sneaking a quick look, he noticed the man had poured himself a drink and sat at the small dining table close to the window. His back was to the window and his head was buried in his hands, as if he was crying.

Santiago scoffed at the man's show of emotion. *Weakling*, he thought.

He bent and tried the window.

Locked, but there was another window at the other end of the fire escape.

He hurried there, tried the window. Unlocked.

Smiling, he grabbed the frame to lift it, but a sudden knock on the condo door had Marino's head snapping up. The man wiped away the trails of tears, and disgust filled Santiago again at the man's weakness.

Marino hurried to the door and opened it, obviously surprised by guests, especially at such a late hour.

Santiago was surprised as well as he recognized Trey Gonzalez from the photos he'd found online. A woman was with him. His sister, Mia, he guessed. She didn't look like the party girl he'd seen in the photos on her social media, but there was no denying she was a beautiful woman. He'd have no issue with doing her before he killed her, he thought, but forced his thoughts away from that to what was happening in the condo.

Whatever the SBS duo said had Marino inviting them into the room. Ever the host, he must have offered them something, but the siblings waved him off.

Santiago couldn't hear from where he was standing but as the three moved to the table where Marino had been sitting earlier, he shifted to listen to their conversation.

Even though he was closer, the sound from the nearby street and the arrival of a garbage truck in the alley behind the building made it hard for him to hear everything. Only bits and pieces of their discussion drifted out, but it was enough to know they were pressing Marino about Ramirez.

Marino, who according to his police mole hadn't said a thing, was saying more now.

"Silent partner…struggle…pandemic."

He hadn't heard Hollywood's name yet but was sure it was coming.

He couldn't let that happen.

Whipping out his gun, he centered himself at the window and opened fire.

For the briefest moment, he squinted against the shattering glass.

A mistake.

Before he could shoot at Marino again, Trey had upended the table for protection and pulled both Marino and his sister behind it.

Stunned, he delayed another dangerous second.

Trey popped up from behind the protection of the table and fired.

The bullet slammed into the body armor beneath his guayabera, stealing his breath, but he forced himself to move.

Turning, he scrambled to the fire escape ladder and raced down, cursing as pain lanced through his leg.

"Call 911," Trey called out and, at the pounding above him, Santiago knew the SBS chief was giving chase.

He fired upward wildly and stumbled down the last few steps on the ladder.

His leg crumpled beneath him as he hit the ground, a lucky thing, otherwise Trey's shot from above might have struck home again.

Cradling an arm against his bruised ribs, he raced around the corner and onto Collins, dodging cars as he hurried across the street.

He didn't look back as he heard the screech of wheels, the crunch of metal and glass, and drivers cursing. His one hope was that Gonzalez was sandwiched between those crashed cars.

As he reached the BMW he had parked by Española Way, he risked a glance back.

No one was following.

Satisfied he was in the clear, he hopped into the BMW and sped off.

Chapter Twenty

Brett had barely laid his head on the couch pillow when his phone vibrated, rattling on the coffee table.

He snatched it up, not wanting to disturb Anita and disturbed enough himself since calls at this hour were never good.

Trey, he realized with a quick glance at the caller ID. He answered the video call.

Trey looked even more tired than before and his hair was disheveled, as if he'd repeatedly run his fingers through it.

"What's up, boss?" he whispered.

"Anita was on the money about Marino. He knew more than he was sharing with the police, but he's sharing now since someone tried to take him out less than an hour ago," Trey advised.

"Kennedy?" he asked, then popped off the couch and started pacing, waking Mango, who had been dozing by the front door. The pit bull popped up her head, instantly alert to the action, but seeing it was him, she laid her head back down on her paws.

"Kennedy. I got a look at him after he fired at Marino," Trey said, but Brett could tell there was more his friend and boss wasn't saying.

"Please tell me you didn't go after him," Brett pleaded, scared that Marielena would grow up without her father.

"I'm fine but Kennedy got away. CCTV tracked him to Española Way and a black BMW. Heath ran the plates, but the car was reported stolen just like the Mercedes he was driving earlier," Trey said with a rough sigh.

"Let me guess. Stolen from one of Hollywood's car lots," he said and angrily wagged his head.

"You got it. But Marino is talking, and Hollywood is definitely involved. Turns out he was a silent partner. Gave Ramirez and Marino a few million in exchange for access to the hotel and all its facilities. Probably to run his bookmaking and sell drugs. In addition, they were supposed to repay him, a million every year, but then the pandemic hit—"

"And all the best-laid plans fell apart," Brett finished for him.

Trey nodded. "Marino admitted that Kennedy had come around a time or two, asking about the money. Apparently, Hollywood thinks they're hiding the profits that should be repaid to him."

"We have our link," Brett considered and wiped a hand across his mouth. "Are you going to share this with the Feds?"

Trey smirked and laughed. "Do you think we should?"

Brett immediately shook his head. "Not unless it's going to be quid pro quo."

"I agree. They're keeping something from us, and we need to know what that is," Trey said and then looked across the room. A second later Mia walked into view and laid a hand on her brother's shoulder.

"I apologize but I'm taking *mi hermanito* home before he falls flat on his face," she said.

"Ten hundred sharp," Trey said as Mia's finger appeared on screen a second before the call ended.

Now that's real progress, he thought, grateful that Anita and he had shared her thoughts about Marino with his SBS colleagues.

And little by little, the case against Kennedy, and Hollywood as well, was getting stronger.

Which meant they were getting closer to ending the threat to Anita's safety.

He should have been happy about that, he thought as he softly padded down to her room and peeked in.

She was sound asleep in a tangle of sheets, her beautiful legs peeking out as she lay on her back. Her dark hair was free of the topknot she normally wore, a dark spill across the electric white of the sheets. Her hand lay outspread, palm open and wide next to her.

How many times had he come to her after a late shift on the base and found her like this. Slipped his hand into hers and woken her. Made love with her.

He hardened in the confines of his jeans and sucked in a breath to control his response.

That slightest noise woke her.

Her eyes fluttered open, and she seemed startled at first, but then relaxed as she realized it was him.

"Everything okay?" she asked and sat up slightly.

The blanket slipped down, exposing her upper body. The thin white fabric of the cheap pajamas did nothing to hide the generous globes of her breasts and darker areolas.

As she realized where his gaze had gone, her nipples tightened into hard points.

He forced himself not to remember how they'd tasted. How she'd moan...

"Everything's okay," he shot out and more calmly added, "You were right about Marino. He knew more than he was saying. Kennedy tried to shut him up, but luckily Trey was there."

Anita snatched the blanket back up in a stranglehold, a reaction to both his gaze and the news. "Trey wasn't hurt, was he?"

He shook his head. "Everyone is fine. They have Kennedy on CCTV fleeing the scene in a black BMW and Marino has implicated Hollywood. The noose is tightening so this will all be over soon," he said and in a softer, sadder tone, added, "You'll be home soon."

ANITA SHOULD HAVE been happy about that.

But she wasn't.

Being home again meant saying goodbye to Brett.

Or did it? she asked herself, her body humming with need from the hungry look he'd given her before he schooled his emotions and walked out the door.

Even now her insides vibrated and dampened as she remembered making love with him. She drifted her hand up over her breast, bit back a moan at the sensitivity of her tight nipples.

He'd always done this to her. Always roused this kind of passion.

Always satisfied as a lover, but as she'd painfully discovered, that alone hadn't been enough.

But as he'd said over and over, he was no longer the same man.

But was he a better man? A man who would stay? she asked herself as she willed passion to subside in her body so she could think clearly.

The answer came immediately.

Yes.

BRETT HAD BARELY settled onto the couch when he heard a footfall in the hallway.

He half rose on the couch and reached for his weapon, but immediately recognized Anita's silhouette in the dim light.

"What's wrong?" he asked and sat up.

She padded over and sat cross-legged on the couch beside him, looking slightly girlish with her loose hair cascading down onto her breasts.

Breasts he instantly pulled his gaze from to avoid an embarrassing reaction she would surely see.

"Earlier tonight you asked if there was hope for us and I said 'maybe.'"

Hopeful emotion choked his throat, making it impossible for him to speak. He tipped his head, urging her to continue.

"I was wrong," she said, making his heart plummet until she shifted and crawled into his lap.

She cupped his jaw and ran a finger across his thick, closely cropped beard. The sound rasped loudly in the quiet of night.

"Anita?" he asked but she laid an index finger across his lips.

"The past is…the past. The last few days…you've shown me what kind of man you've become, and while you're not perfect—"

"Ouch," he muttered against her finger.

"I'm not, either," she admitted with a siren's smile.

Being this close to her, with the woman he'd loved and wanted for so long, made it impossible to curb his need any longer. Especially as she snuggled close, bringing her warm center directly above his hardness.

He swept his hands to her hips to urge her even closer and she moaned and pressed herself to him.

"Brett," she rasped.

"I want you. I want this, whatever this is," he said, afraid to say the four-letter word he suspected she wanted to hear most.

"I'm a big girl. I'll take whatever this is," Anita said, then bent her head and kissed him.

Her consent released the hunger he'd been holding in check.

He ripped the thin cotton nightshirt from her body, exposing her to his gaze. Cradling her breast, he rubbed his thumb across her hard nipple and whispered, "You are so beautiful. More beautiful than I remembered."

She followed his lead, fumbling for a second before yanking his T-shirt away.

A shocked gasp filled the air and she gently, almost reverently, skipped her fingers across the silvery and hard ridges across his upper chest.

"Do they hurt?" she asked, voice tight with emotion.

He shook his head. "Not anymore."

IT WAS IMPOSSIBLE not to think about how he must have suffered, she thought as she traced the uneven ridges scattered across his upper body. Slightly lower there was a longer, smoother but clearly man-made scar. A physician's handiwork, and she shuddered at the thought that she might have lost him permanently so many years ago.

He tucked his thumb and forefinger beneath her chin and gently urged her gaze to his. She waited for him to say something. Anything. Instead, he just tenderly brushed back a lock of stray hair and kissed her.

A whisper-light kiss. An invitation and not a demand.

She accepted, opening her mouth to his. Dancing her tongue with his as he cradled her breast and teased the tip.

She wanted his mouth on her. Wanted him buried deep inside as she shifted her hips against him, and he groaned and pushed upward.

In the dance of partners familiar with each other, he cradled her breasts together and kissed her, shifting from one tip to the other, until he suckled on one and nearly sent her over the edge.

"Please, Brett," she keened, and he shot to his feet, cradling her against his chest.

At the front door, Mango jumped to her feet and growled, misunderstanding his action.

With a hand signal, he confirmed the command with, "*Lehni*, Mango. *Lehni.*"

The dog hesitated but lay down.

"Good girl, Mango. *Pozor*," he said, commanding her to guard the door.

Mango settled in at the entrance, head on her paws.

He pushed forward to his bedroom, laid her on the bed and

quickly stripped off his jeans. He slowed only long enough to remove his wallet and a condom he set on the nightstand.

As he climbed on the bed beside her, facing her, she once again explored his body, trailing her hand across his upper chest and down the long scar she hated seeing. She kept on going until she'd encircled him, and he sucked in a breath.

"You like?" she asked, feeling like a temptress.

He laughed and cupped her breast. Tweaked the hard nipple.

Now it was her turn to gasp as that tug ripped straight to her center.

"You like?" he teased, a boyish grin on his face before he bent and took the tip into his mouth.

When he sucked on it, she nearly lost it, but she bit her lip and cupped the back of his skull, urging him on while stroking him with her other hand.

The years of separation slipped away as they made love. Moves both familiar and yet also unexpected lifted desire to heights she hadn't experienced before until she was on the edge, barely hanging on.

He shifted inside her, driving her ever higher, and she called out his name, drawing his gaze to her face.

The words nearly slipped from her then. Nearly, but it was too soon. Too uncertain.

"It's okay, Anita. It's okay," he said as if aware of what she was keeping hidden, protected, deep in her heart.

But while the words wouldn't come, she splayed her hand over his heart and held on as he drove them ever higher until they both held their breath, poised on the precipice.

With one last stroke, he pushed them over and they fell together to the bed, joined. Wrapped in each other's arms.

Chapter Twenty-One

They woke tangled together, peaceful until Mango's growl had Brett flying from the bed naked.

He rushed to the coffee table and grabbed his gun as Mango rose and faced the front door, another low rumble coming from her throat.

Peering through the peephole, he realized it was Jake's neighbor and instructed Mango to sit down.

Tucking the gun behind him, he unlocked the door and opened it, staying behind it to hide his nudity.

"Mornin', Jim."

"Mornin', Brett. Sorry to wake you so early, but I thought you should know that I noticed a red Jeep driving by a few times. Seemed a little suspicious to me," the old man said.

Brett dipped his head in thanks, grateful for the retired cop's eagle eyes. "Any chance you have a video camera that might have picked it up?"

Jim shook his head. "Don't believe in all that new technology. I like my privacy," he said and, with a wave of his hand, turned and walked away.

Too bad, he thought.

It was also too bad that the video doorbell on Jake's house didn't face the street. At best the camera might have gotten only a sliver of anything passing by. Still, a sliver was better than nothing.

Since he'd helped Jake set up the camera and sometimes stayed there, he had access to the recorded videos.

Sure enough, the history showed that a red Jeep Wrangler had passed by the house in the early-morning hours. It had gone east, then west, then east again, toward the homes at the end of the canal. If it was just another neighbor, the car should be parked somewhere along this street or the perpendicular cul-de-sac at the end.

A quick walk with Mango would confirm that.

Anita slipped her arms around his waist, surprising him and making him jump.

He cursed and faced her. "You snuck up on me."

"You were lost in thought," she said and rose on tiptoe to brush a kiss on his lips, her naked body flush against his, rousing desire that he had to tamp down.

"Who was at the door?" she asked.

"Jim. It was nothing," he assured her and quickly tacked on, "We have a meeting in about an hour and I don't know about you, but I need some coffee and food." He rubbed his belly in emphasis.

She stroked the back of her hand across his stomach and laughed. "Man cannot live on love alone, right?"

The moment had been relatively lighthearted, but turned serious with what should have been playful words.

Stammering, he jerked his thumb in the direction of the kitchen. "How about I make some coffee while you shower—"

"And I'll cook breakfast while you clean up," she finished for him.

ANITA NODDED AND rushed off to shower. Alone. Thankfully.

Showering with Brett, which she'd done dozens of times in the past, would have been way too intimate now.

Way more intimate than what you already did all night long? the little voice in her head challenged, but she shushed it.

I won't apologize for having needs.

Needs? the voice chided but she ignored it and hurried into the shower. Washing quickly, she dried off and dashed to her bedroom to dress. She wouldn't have much time to make breakfast and clean up before the meeting with the rest of the SBS crew.

As she entered the kitchen, he handed her a mug. "I hope I got it right."

She sipped it, then nodded and smiled, pleased that he'd remembered how she took her coffee. "Perfect."

With that, he almost ran down the hall and her heart sank with the awkwardness between them this morning.

What did you expect? the annoying voice chimed in.

She ignored it, focusing on the delicious, perfectly made mug of coffee and the breakfast she had to prepare.

With the clock ticking away, she played it safe with blueberry pancakes, breakfast sausage and warm maple syrup. She normally wouldn't have bought the premade sausage, but she had remembered that Brett liked it and impulsively grabbed some while they'd been shopping.

Brett returned barely fifteen minutes later, dressed in khaki shorts and a pale yellow guayabera like those so many men wore in Miami. The pale color emphasized the cocoa brown of his beard, hair and eyes.

He went to the fridge and took out fresh food for Mango, dished it out and refilled her water bowl. He called the pit bull over, and Mango gobbled the food down so fast, Anita worried the dog might choke. But when she finished and drank deeply from the water bowl, she returned to her spot by the front door.

When Brett passed by her to grab place mats and cutlery, he laid a possessive hand at her waist and dropped a kiss on her cheek, alleviating some of the morning's earlier self-consciousness.

With a quick toss of the pan, she flipped the pancake, earning a "Show-off" from him.

She chuckled and winked. "Jealous much?"

He responded with a laugh and finished setting the bistro table as she placed a stack of pancakes on their plates and added the sausage. He took those over to the table while she poured warm maple syrup into a small jug for serving.

Because time was short, breakfast was relatively silent except for appreciative murmurs from Brett. When the plates were empty of everything but some scattered crumbs and a few drops of maple syrup, they worked together to clean and prepare for their meeting.

Barely five minutes later, they were staring at the SBS team.

"You look a little better than you did last night," Brett said. The smudges beneath his friend's eyes were not as deep and his skin had a little more color.

"Some sleep and a visit to Roni and the baby this morning worked some magic," he said and, for good measure, shared a picture of mama and baby.

Everyone around the table responded with congrats again, but then Trey quickly turned the conversation over to Sophie and Robbie's report.

"As Trey advised, CCTV picked up on Kennedy's escape after he tried to kill Marino. The police sent us the footage and we were able to trace the passage of the vehicle using an assortment of traffic cameras and ALPRs. The BMW headed south. We lost it in the Homestead area," Sophie said, worry on her engaging features, so much like Trey's and Mia's that there was no denying they were cousins.

"You think he's headed here?" Brett pressed, brows rising in question.

"Possibly," Robbie advised and continued. "An ALPR at a traffic light last picked up the BMW on Route 1. There is a BOLO out for Kennedy and the vehicle so hopefully either a sharp-eyed officer or another ALPR will see it."

"But you're sure it was a black BMW?" he asked, mindful of what Jim had seen and the footage on Jake's doorbell video.

"Positive but be mindful Kennedy may have already dumped the Bimmer and secured another vehicle," Trey warned.

"Roger that. What about Marino and the Feds? Any progress?" he pushed.

"We're waiting for a complete report from Williams, but he texted to say that Marino has implicated both Kennedy and Hollywood in various crimes. As for the Feds, it seems there's been a change in their attitude, possibly because they don't want the local LEOs to get sole credit for apprehending a high-profile target like Hollywood," Trey said.

"Sounds good. Is it okay if I send you some footage from our video doorbell?" he asked.

"Something hinky?" Trey asked, espresso-colored brows furrowing.

"Maybe or it could be nothing. Jake's neighbor is a retired cop and noticed a suspicious red Jeep Wrangler. Our doorbell picked up the vehicle, but it's at a bad angle. I was hoping Sophie and Robbie could take a look."

"Send it over," Sophie immediately said.

"Will do," he confirmed.

Trey did a quick glance around the table to see if anyone else had anything to say and when all remained silent, he said, "We'll be in touch as soon as we have more."

When he ended the call, Anita leaned close and said, "Jim saw something?"

He didn't want to worry her, so he said, "It could just be a retired cop seeing things that aren't there."

"Or his expert eyes really picked up on something," she said and splayed her fingers on the countertop, as if trying to stabilize her world.

He laid his hand on hers and squeezed. "Let me send the video to Sophie and Robbie and see what they make of it."

Chapter Twenty-Two

Anita hoped that the SBS tech gurus would be able to allay their fears, but she was too anxious to just sit and wait for a reply.

Gesturing to Mango, she asked, "Is it time to take her for a walk?"

He nodded. "Now is a good time. That red Jeep headed toward the cul-de-sac at the end of the canal. Could just be someone heading home."

She hoped he was right and trusted that he would make the right decisions to keep her safe.

They walked to the front door, where he grabbed Mango's leash and clipped it on. He opened the door but said, "Hold on while I check."

He went ahead, Mango at his side, inspected the side and front yard and then doubled back to let her know it was clear.

Outside, they strolled to the street, still as quiet as it had been the day before. He assumed the position closest to the road, Mango between them, as they leisurely walked down the block, heading for the cul-de-sac to find the red Jeep, hopefully parked in front of the owner's home.

As they reached the end of the block, she peered down the street and pointed. "There it is," she said.

BRETT HAD SEEN the vehicle also. It was on the east side of the cul-de-sac in front of a small ranch-style home. Directly opposite that home was a row of tall, thick oleanders, flush with pink flowers, forming a dense border along another home's yard.

Too dense.

Someone could easily be hiding behind those bushes.

Because of that, he shifted to the other side of the street, the one where the Jeep was stationed, and directed Anita to the inside, away from the street and those possibly dangerous bushes.

He approached the Jeep, but nothing seemed out of order. For safety's sake, he snapped off a photo of the license plate so Sophie and Robbie could check to see who owned it.

Swiveling around, he inspected the area, but all was quiet.

Gesturing to the other end of the street, he said, "Let's finish our walk and get back to the house."

SANTIAGO CLIMBED OVER the short fence and hurried down the dock, working his way toward the house where he suspected Mr. Brett Madison was guarding the chef who could ID him.

After getting the name from his FBI contact, he'd searched the internet and, although Mr. Brett Madison had done an excellent job of scrubbing himself from most places, he'd found an article that the *Marine Corps Times* had done when several marine units had helped distribute food in the Philippines after a typhoon had caused extensive devastation.

He'd recognized Madison immediately, although he'd been several years younger. The photo had shown him, SBS Chief Trey Gonzalez and fellow marine Jacob Benjamin Anderson.

Jacob, apparently known as Jake to his friends, hadn't been as careful as Gonzalez and Madison.

Social media content galore and easily found via a free online phone book.

Just a few more houses, Santiago thought, but then he caught sight of the old man sitting on a lawn chair farther down the dock that ran behind the homes.

Even though he was older, the man was still in good shape.

Whipcord lean muscles warned he'd put up quite a fight. Worse, he had that look about him. Either ex-cop or ex-military and he was directly in the way of him reaching his destination.

He could fight him or even just shoot him, but that would alert Madison to trouble.

That was the last thing he wanted to do. He needed the element of surprise if he was going to be able to overcome Madison and that powerful pit bull.

With a nonchalant wave at the man, he doubled back to where he'd parked the Jeep. He'd return later, when it was dark and easier to avoid prying eyes.

He hopped the fence again and raced across the last yard and around the thick row of oleanders.

As he slipped into the Jeep, he couldn't believe what he was seeing right in front of him.

Madison, the woman and that damn dog.

They were at the far end of the cul-de-sac and boxed in by cars on either side of the street.

Perfect, he thought, then started the car and gunned the engine.

Chapter Twenty-Three

Brett whirled around at the sound of the racing engine.

The Jeep was barreling toward them, but they were at the end of the street and cars lined either side, leaving no room for escape. But at their end of the block a wide swath of dock ran perpendicular to the street along the waters of another canal.

"Run," he said, urging Anita in the direction of the dock and scooping up Mango.

At the edge of the narrow dock, Anita hesitated.

He wrapped an arm around her and hauled her close as he jumped into the water.

SANTIAGO SCREECHED TO a stop, cursing and hitting the steering wheel in frustration as he watched the trio leap into the canal.

He raced out of the Jeep and ran to the edge of the dock, but he couldn't see them in the waters below.

That didn't stop him from opening fire into the canal.

He emptied his clip, but as people raced out of their homes, he couldn't linger.

He raced back to the Jeep, reversed down the block and, with a quick K-turn, sped away.

MANGO FOUGHT AGAINST HIM, clawing to be free of the water.

Anita started to rise, but he laid a hand on her shoulder and kept her down.

She looked at him, fearful eyes wide against the stinging seawater, and he gestured upward.

Above them bullets pierced the surface and flew downward, creating deadly trails in the water.

When the last of the bullets swam by, he pushed off the bottom and to the surface. Anita popped up next to him a second later.

He released Mango, who immediately began dog-paddling beside him as Brett searched for some way to reach the dock again.

Suddenly, Jim leaned over the edge of the dock and held out his hand. "Heard the commotion and came to help," he said.

Brett grabbed hold of Jim's hand and that of another neighbor who had also come to assist. The two men boosted him up easily and, in turn, he bent to lift Anita out of the water.

"You're not hurt, are you?" he asked, inspecting Anita as she stood beside him.

"I'm fine," she said.

Jim lifted Mango out of the water and deposited her on the dock.

The dog shook her body, sending water everywhere, and then immediately came to Brett's side and bumped his leg with her head, almost as if in apology.

Her thick nails had torn his shirt and raked deep scratches into his chest as she'd struggled against him underwater, fear gripping her.

"You're a good girl, Mango," he said and rubbed her head and ears.

The sound of approaching sirens perked up Mango's ears, and barely a minute later, a squad car came around the corner and parked.

Brett had wanted to keep a low profile but clearly that would no longer be possible.

"Neighbors probably called 911," Jim said as he looked at the cruiser.

Brett nodded. His mind raced with all the possible things he could do to protect Anita now that this location was also blown.

One immediately came to mind. Turning to the old cop, he said, "Could you do me a favor?"

Jim bowed his head and said, "Sure. What is it?"

Not wanting others to overhear, he leaned close and whispered his request to the older man.

"Got it. I'll reach out to Jake and be waiting for you," he said and pushed off, hurrying past the police officer with a quick salute.

Anita stood shivering beside him, but a fifty-something female walked over and wrapped a beach towel around her. "Th-th-thank y-y-ou," Anita said past her chattering lips.

"No worries, honey. Keep it," the woman said and handed Brett another towel to dry down.

Not that it would take long. Even though it was December, the sun was strong and the day warm. Already in the low seventies, if he had to guess.

Anita's trembling was likely more from fear than cold.

He wrapped an arm around her and rubbed his hand up and down her side, offering support and reassurance as they answered the volley of questions the officer, a young Latino man named Hernandez, was asking.

Names, addresses and their business in the area. A description of the car, which also had Brett pulling out his cell phone to provide the license plate number. Officer Hernandez jotted it all down and was about to start asking even more questions when his radio chirped to life.

"Hernandez here," he said as he answered.

"Miami PD wants your report and said to release the victims ASAP," the dispatcher advised.

"10-4. We're done here anyway," Hernandez said and faced them.

"You heard. You're free to go. Do you need a ride?" he asked.

Brett flipped a hand in the direction of the street off the cul-de-sac. "We're just a few doors down."

The officer nodded and headed to his patrol car while Anita, Mango and he rushed down the block. But the officer, obviously aware that this was an unusual and dangerous situation, followed them in his cruiser and parked in front of Jake's house.

Brett walked Anita toward the entrance of the side yard and door and said, "Wait here."

Hurrying back to the cruiser, he leaned down and said, "This guy won't hesitate to shoot, so stay vigilant."

The young officer nodded. "10-4. Do you need an escort to somewhere else?"

Brett peered toward the SUV in the driveway. He had no doubt it had already been compromised by Kennedy noting the plate number. They had no idea how many dirty cops Kennedy had in his pocket who would use the ALPRs to track their travel.

He shook his head. "We're going to stay here for now," he said, even though he had no plans to do that.

"I'll be sure to drive past here often while I'm on patrol," he said.

"That would be appreciated," Brett said and tapped his hand on the window frame to let the officer know he was good to go.

Hands on hips, he watched the officer drive away, did another quick look around the property and then walked with Mango back toward the side yard and door.

As he had so many times before, he opened the door and sent Mango ahead to scope out the house.

Not that he expected Kennedy to have lingered there after trying to run them down.

But he had no doubt Kennedy would be back, which meant they had to be on the move as soon as possible.

Inside, he turned to Anita, who stood in the dining room,

shaking even with the towel and her arms wrapped around herself.

He laid a hand on her shoulder and cupped her cheek. Leaning down so she couldn't avoid his gaze, he said, "It's going to be okay. Take a warm shower and pack up your things. We'll be on the move as soon as I talk to Trey."

She nodded and walked down the hall, and he pulled out a fresh burner phone and called Trey.

"Are you all okay?" Trey asked, clearly having been filled in by MPD.

"Pretty much," Brett said and peered at the angry scrapes on his chest that were stinging from the salt water in the canal.

Trey released a colorful stream of curses about the state of things and Brett had to agree. "Yes, it's totally messed up. We can't stay here, it's compromised."

"I agree. I'm looking for another place for you—"

"No need, Trey. I have an idea," he said and relayed the plan that had occurred to him.

"Unorthodox, but it makes sense," Trey said with a low whistle.

"How did he find us? I thought you had plugged the leak at PD," Brett pressed, angry that another location had been compromised.

"I don't know but I have my suspicions, particularly since the FBI is finally involved in this," his friend said.

"You think the leak is there?" Brett asked, not that the FBI agents were so far beyond reproach.

"Possibly. Williams, Roni and I are going to speak with the lead Fed. Alone. In the meantime, go ahead with your plan. I'll reach out to you later once we've finished," Trey said.

"Roger that," he said and ended the call.

THE SHOWER HAD helped immensely to chase away the fear of the moment and the salt water of the canal.

And as she'd shoved her meager belongings into a plastic bag, anger replaced fear. Determination replaced worry.

She marched out to the dining room where Brett had just finished his call.

"What can I do?" she asked, chin tilted up defiantly.

But as Trey turned in her direction, she gasped and walked over to him to gently brush aside the torn fabric of his shirt. "Oh my god. We need to tend to those," she said, shocked by the deep, angry scratches on his chest.

"Mango panicked underwater, but I couldn't let her stay on the dock. Kennedy would have shot her," he said in explanation.

Anita bobbed her head in agreement. "I get it. Why don't you shower, and after, I'll get those cleaned and bandaged."

"Thanks. We're leaving here. Would you mind packing up our food supplies? Nothing too perishable."

"I'll get them ready," she said and hurried to do as he asked, mentally preparing a menu from the foods they had and which would keep for a few days.

She carefully packed things away and then returned to her bathroom and searched the cabinet for disinfectant, antibiotic ointment, gauze and tape.

Brett exited his bedroom bare-chested and wearing unbuttoned jeans that hung loose on his lean hips, toweling dry his high-and-tight hair.

Lord, but he was gorgeous, even with his warrior's scars.

Her heart pounded with need, but also that fear again that she'd almost lost him forever.

Juggling the items to tend to the scratches, she said, "Why don't you sit on the couch."

When he did so, legs splayed wide, she slipped between his powerful thighs and sat opposite him on the coffee table. She laid out her first aid supplies, applied disinfectant to some gauze and swiped it across the scratches to clean them.

His muscles jumped beneath her ministrations, but he didn't move otherwise.

With fresh gauze, she applied the antibiotic ointment and then taped more gauze in place over the scratches.

"Did you pack up?" he asked when she'd finished, and he offered her a hand up from the coffee table.

She motioned to the assortment of bags on the floor by the kitchen counter. "All ready to go."

He smiled, waggled his head and said, "I'll be back."

He sauntered down the hall, popped into his bedroom and exited a second later, shrugging on a fresh guayabera, the duffel with his clothes in hand.

When he reached her, he stuffed her clothes into the duffel and slung it on his shoulder. After, he filled his hands with a number of the bags she'd packed and she did the same, grabbing as many as she could. Mango helped out as well, picking up a smaller bag with her mouth.

She followed Brett to the back door, where he paused and peered out.

Looking back at her, he said, "We're good to go."

Chapter Twenty-Four

When they stepped outside, she realized Jim was by their dock, a shotgun cradled in his arms. The boat that had previously been high up on the lift had been lowered into the water, where it bobbed gently in the canal.

"Was Jake cool with us taking the boat?" He'd asked Jim to call his friend for permission to use the boat and, if it was okay, prep it.

"He is," Jim said with a dip of his head.

"Thanks, Jim," Brett said and clapped Jim on the back.

The older man nodded and handed him the shotgun. "You might need this," he said and added, "Put a box of shells in the console glove box."

"Thanks again. I truly appreciate it," he said and shook the other man's hand. It was then he noticed the Semper Fi tattooed on the man's forearm.

"Anything for a fellow marine," he said, then turned to Anita and jabbed a finger in her direction.

"You take care of him and you," Jim said with another determined point.

"Good man," she said and watched him walk away in the direction of his house.

"Yes, he is," Brett agreed, then laid his bags on the deck and gently placed the shotgun against the nearest console on the boat. He turned, reached across for her bags and put them on the deck of the boat as well. Finished loading the bags, he asked, "Did you take Mango's food also?"

"Of course. I would never forget Mango," she said and kneeled to pet the dog, who had been patiently sitting on the dock beside her.

Smiling, he held out a hand to help her onto the boat. She stumbled a little as the boat rocked and laid a hand over her stomach, as if a little nauseous already.

"It'll be better once we move. There is a sleeping area, galley and head down below," he said and opened the cockpit door, familiar with the boat from his father's catalogs and having rented similar vessels.

"I'll get these supplies put away," she said, then grabbed some of the bags and disappeared through the opening to belowdecks.

Brett picked up the shotgun and placed it at the cockpit door, just in case. He checked the console for the shells and, satisfied they were in easy reach, stowed his gun there as well to keep it dry but easily accessible. He hopped back onto the dock and signaled Mango to heel as he returned to Jake's house and went into a pantry where he had noticed a big-box-store-sized package of bottled water.

He hoisted that in one hand, locked up the house and returned to the boat.

Mango didn't follow him down, remaining on the dock, where she paced almost nervously. Unusual for the normally fearless dog, and he wondered if she was associating the boat and nearby waters with the scary moments she had experienced not that long ago.

"Come on, Mango. *Kemne*," he urged, instructing her to come onto the boat. She hesitated and he repeated the command. *"Kemne."*

This time she finally hopped up and over the side, her feet

skidding on the smooth surface amidships as she landed on the deck.

"Good girl," he said and stroked her head. He caught sight of a familiar package through the thin plastic bag, reached in and took out Mango's treats. He handed her one and further reinforced her behavior with another rub of her head.

"Lehni," he instructed, and she immediately lay down, sprawling in the middle of the deck. He was grateful for her quick response because he had to be able to rely on her following her commands without hesitation.

He snatched up the last of the bags and took them down to the galley, where Anita was unpacking and stowing items in the cabinets. She turned as he entered and said, "The fridge isn't working."

Nodding, he said, "It probably needs the engine running or a solar panel for power. We'll figure it out once we're underway."

He returned topside for the bottled water, brought it down to her and then went back up to untie the boat.

Anita came up then. "I'll get the bumpers," she said, reminding him that she'd sometimes gone boating with her father.

"Thanks," he said, and as he maneuvered away from the dock, she pulled up the bumpers that protected the boat from dock damage and stowed them beneath the seats at the stern.

She stepped over Mango, who hadn't moved, and joined him at the console.

Laying a hand on his shoulder, she asked, "Where are we going?"

"Jake and I used to go fishing in this area and sometimes stay overnight. There's an anchorage spot near Islamorada and Shell Key that's perfect for tonight," he said, carefully steering the boat to the end of their canal. He turned away from the spot where they'd had to jump into the water.

He cruised wide past that area slowly, keeping an eye out for anything untoward, and caught sight of a police cruiser doing a K-turn on that block.

Officer Hernandez, patrolling as he'd promised.

Brett drove ahead sluggishly, aware of the no-wake zone in the canal area, but as soon as he cleared the last bit of canal, he pushed the boat to its top speed, heading for the Atlantic Intracoastal Waterway and Cowpens Cut. That channel would let them navigate down the Intracoastal and to the familiar spot where they could anchor. Maybe even fish for dinner.

He kept an eye on the boat's radar to make sure he was avoiding any of the shallow shoals or reefs in the area.

"You seem comfortable with this," she said and slipped onto the seat opposite him. Surprisingly, Mango hopped up into her lap, dragging a laugh from her.

"You are so not a lapdog," she said as Mango insinuated herself into the tight space between Anita and the padded console in front of her.

"Mango. Get down. *Lehni*," he called out, but the dog remained in Anita's lap, worrying him, but he didn't press since it seemed to reassure Anita.

IT'S OKAY. REALLY. She's not too heavy," Anita said and rubbed the dog's head as she sat there, tongue lolling out of her mouth. A cooling breeze bathed them as the boat moved along, and Anita raised her head to catch the air, much like Mango was doing.

If she hadn't been on the run for her life, she might have appreciated the lovely views of the bright cerulean waters, darker in spots from the reefs below, or the lush, verdant foliage and expensive homes along the shore.

It didn't take long to reach what she supposed was Cowpens Cut.

Mangrove and underbrush marked the edges of the narrow strait while channel markers warned of the depth in the center.

Blue-green waters also identified the navigable areas in the middle while white sand was visible beneath the shallow waters along the edges of the cut.

It was a short trip through the area, and once he'd cleared it, Brett increased the boat's speed, following the buoys and channel markers that identified the path for the Intracoastal Waterway.

"That's Plantation Key over there," Brett said and gestured eastward to a larger collection of homes and land along the spit of sand and highway that made up the Keys.

"Will it take long to reach Islamorada?" she asked, unfamiliar with these waters. When she'd gone out with her father, they'd stayed in Biscayne Bay.

"Not long. We should be there in about an hour. Once we get there, we'll anchor and see if there are solar panels we can set up to power the fridge, appliances and the lights for tonight," he said, his gaze constantly traveling along the route and also peering back, making sure all was good.

"What about Trey? Can we reach him out here?" she asked, worried about cell reception, not that they were all that far from land.

"We have service where we anchor even though it's not all that close to shore. I'll call as soon as we're anchored and set up for power."

As PROMISED, it wasn't long before they had reached their destination.

In one of the storage areas, Brett located solar panels and cables that connected to a battery array on the boat. In a second area along the hull of the boat, he found rods, reels and Jake's tackle box, filled with lures and other necessities.

He quickly set up the solar panels and plugged them in to power the appliances and provide light at night. Once he'd done that, he pulled out the rods, reels and tackle box and brought them to a bait station at the stern.

"I thought we might fish for our meal," he said, thinking that the task would also distract Anita from thinking about what had happened just hours earlier.

He was about to help her assemble the tackle, but she went into action without hesitation. "This is old hat to me. My *papi* didn't cut me and my sister any slack when we went fishing."

"Good to know. Since you can handle that, I'm going to call Trey," he said, then pulled out the burner phone and walked around the cockpit area to the bow of the boat. He climbed up onto the seats there and perused the area, vigilant for any danger.

There were several pleasure craft out on the waters, but none seemed to be heading in their direction. Feeling secure, he dialed Trey.

"Have you anchored?" he asked as soon as he answered.

"We have. Everything seems secure for now," Brett advised and did another slow swivel to scope out the area around Shell Key.

"Good. We spoke to the FBI agent handling the Hollywood investigation. He admitted that they'd suspected they had a leak on their team since Hollywood kept slipping through their fingers every time they got close," Trey advised.

Brett blew out a breath, shook his head and drove a hand through his hair. "Is that why they didn't want to cooperate?"

"Yes. They were afraid the leak could compromise our investigation, which had made more progress than theirs," his friend reported.

"And now? Why the change in their attitude?" Brett wondered. He hopped off the seat cushion and walked back to the stern, where Anita had their poles all set to go.

He sauntered to her and said, "I'm putting the phone on speaker."

"Great," Trey said and continued with his report. "The FBI had their suspicions on who the leak was and, with all that was happening, upped their surveillance. That caught one of their agents sending your name to what turned out to be a burner phone. The agent confessed that he had sent it to Kennedy."

"And Kennedy somehow connected me to Jake? Is that possible?" he asked.

"I doubted it, too, but I put Sophie and Robbie on it, and they instantly got a hit in a marines newsletter that's also posted online. Jake, you and me were identified in the photo and Jake's info—"

"Is readily available online," Brett finished for him.

"What do we do now?" Anita asked. He noticed the worry lines across her forehead.

An awkward silence followed until Trey said, "The accused FBI agent lawyered up, but he's willing to assist us in exchange for a lighter sentence. We're working on a plan to draw out Kennedy."

Brett didn't like the sound of that at all. "Draw out. Like in a trap?" he asked just to confirm.

That long, pregnant hesitation came again. "Yes, as in a trap."

"And we're the bait?" Anita shot out, obviously understanding exactly what they were planning.

"I'm not a fan of this, either, but it's local cops and the FBI in charge and making the decisions. But I'm not going to hang you out to dry. I'll call in Matt, Natalie and their canines, as well as several of our other agents, to safeguard you," Trey said, his conviction clear.

Brett and Anita gazed at each other, and as one they nodded, trusting Trey. "Whatever you need so we can close this case and Anita can get back to her life," Brett said.

"I'll call at 0900 with an update," Trey said before disconnecting.

Chapter Twenty-Five

Anita didn't know why the thought of returning to her old life saddened her, but she bit her lip and fought off that emotion.

When the call ended, Brett powered down the phone and laid a hand on her shoulder. "Trey will keep his promise. You'll be home soon. Back at the restaurant and with your family well before Christmas."

She forced a smile and bobbed her head up. "I know. It's just that…"

She couldn't finish. Stepping against him, she leaned into this comforting strength. He was like the proverbial oak, strong and steady, but also flexible enough to move as he'd had to with each challenge that had arisen.

He wrapped his arms around her and rocked her gently, comforting her, murmuring over and over that she would be fine. That everything would turn out okay.

She made herself believe that. Repeated it to herself as she stepped away and picked up a rod to distract herself from everything that was happening.

"We have a few hours before it gets dark. Should be enough time to catch something. We usually have luck in this area," Brett said and took hold of the second reel.

Since it seemed like he wanted to keep things chill, she asked, "What do you normally catch here?"

"Snapper, hogfish or snook. Sometimes mahi-mahi," he said.

"All good-eating fish," she said. She reeled in some line and, after releasing the bale arm, did an overhead cast that sent the lure flying out into the waters.

"Good cast. Your *papi* taught you well," he said and playfully clapped her on the back.

"He'd be happy to hear you say that," she said, not intending to return things to serious mode and yet that's where it went.

After a long moment during which Brett cast out his line, he said, "I'd like to meet your *papi* someday. Your *mami*. Maybe your *hermanita*, too. Are you the oldest?"

"I am," she said, but couldn't risk a look at him, afraid of what he might see. Instead, she reeled in her line slowly, hoping for a bite. Anything to keep from looking over at him. To keep it from getting more personal.

She was about to give up on a bite and reel the line in more quickly, but a sharp tug followed by a second stronger hit had her instinctively jerking the rod back to hopefully set the hook.

It worked.

Suddenly a fish came flying out of the water, battling against being hooked. The powerful surge of its leap nearly unbalanced her, but Brett was immediately there, his big body behind her. Hands at her waist to help steady her.

"It's a big tarpon," he said, laughter and surprise in his voice.

Tarpons were known for the fight they put up, Anita knew. Her father had snagged one many years earlier and had spent some time working the fish up to the boat, battling the many leaps and runs the fish had made.

Today was no different.

Over and over the silvery body of the tarpon shot out of the water, leaping and thrashing, its large scales flashing silver in the sunshine. A rattling noise from the fish's gills escaped with each leap.

Mango, hearing the commotion, had hopped up and placed

her front legs on the edges of the stern, watching the leaps and the two of them battling to bring in the big fish.

Anita's arms ached from fighting the jerk and tug of the line and the constant reeling. Sweat dripped down her back and her legs ached, but she had Brett's support behind her, urging her on until she was finally able to reel the tired fish close.

They leaned over to examine the tarpon as it rested on the surface behind the boat, sucking in air through its big mouth, a trait unique to the almost prehistoric fish.

"I'm guessing it's about thirty inches long," Brett said with a low whistle, then whipped out his phone, turned it on and snapped a photo.

At her puzzled look, he said, "So you can show your dad. Tarpon are catch-and-release only."

The catch-and-release made sense. A beautiful warrior like this deserved to go free, she thought.

Just like you have to let Brett go? the little voice in her head challenged.

This investigation may have hooked him into being with her, but she had no doubt that Brett was free to make his own decisions, much like she was.

Brett bent and gently worked the lure out of the tarpon's mouth. He cradled it gently in the water, letting it rest and recover in his hands after the ferocious fight. As soon as the fish seemed to have more energy, he released the tarpon and it slowly swam off, silvery body gliding along the surface for a few feet until it dived and became a dark blue blur speeding away underwater.

Body trembling from the fight, she sat down on one of the cushioned seats behind the console. "I'm beat," she said and wiped some sweat from her brow with the back of her arm.

Brett nodded and smiled. "Understandable. I guess it's up to me to catch our supper," he said and cast out his line.

Mango had remained by the stern, but seemingly bored with what was happening, the pit bull lay down by her feet.

Anita bent and stroked the dog's body, and Mango rolled over to present her belly for a rub. She did, giving her a good massage with both hands. But as she did so, it occurred to her that they had no way to walk the pit bull.

Rising, she strode to Brett's side, careful to avoid the line as he cast. Watching him from the side of her eye, she asked, "How will we walk Mango?"

Brett risked a quick glance back at the pittie, who had risen to watch them as they stood at the stern. "She's trained to go on command. I'll take her up front to relieve herself. Mind taking the rod?"

"Sure," she said and accepted the rod while Brett went below and came back with a plastic bag and some paper towels.

"*Kemne*, Mango," he said and swayed his palm toward him in command.

Mango immediately obeyed, following him toward the bow.

A tug on her line dragged Anita's attention back to fishing.

She tried to set the hook, and when she had a stronger tug and slight run on the line, she knew she had possibly snared dinner. Not a tarpon, she could tell from the way the fish stayed underwater, fighting against the line.

When Brett returned with Mango barely a few minutes later, she handed him the rod, too tired to finish hauling in the fish.

Mango and she stood at the stern and watched Brett work the line, slowly maneuvering the fish closer and closer until he finally brought it to the stern. He leaned over, hooked his fingers into the fish's gills and hauled it onboard.

"Lane snapper, luckily. We're out of season for red snapper," he said as the nice-sized fish flopped around on the floor of the boat.

"Excellent eating. Do you want to prep it or should I?" she asked, but even as she said it, the loud sound of an engine approaching had them both turning.

A Boston Whaler headed straight for them at breakneck speed.

Chapter Twenty-Six

Brett swept his arm in front of Anita and urged her behind him. "Go below," he said, unsure whether the approaching boat was friend or foe.

As Anita hurried away, he slowly backed toward the cockpit door as well to grab the shotgun.

But as he reached for it, the Boston Whaler slowed. As it did so, the bow dipped slightly, allowing him to see the khaki-clad person at the wheel, wearing a familiar drab green baseball cap and black life vest.

Trusting his gut that it really was a game warden patrol boat, he walked back toward the stern of the boat, waiting for the other vessel to pull closer.

The craft slowed and tossed out large white bumpers to protect the two boats from bashing into each other. As they did so, he caught sight of two game wardens, one at the wheel and another at the stern. A large gold star in a circle with the FWC's name sat on a large green vertical stripe on the side of the boat along with the words "Florida Wildlife Commission State Law Enforcement."

"Mind us seeing what you have there?" the officer at the stern asked.

"Feel free," Brett said and waved at the officer to come aboard.

The FWC warden did just that, agilely hopping from his boat to theirs.

"Nice-looking snapper," the warden said, hands on his hips.

"A keeper from what I can see," Brett said with a bob of his head.

The officer nodded in agreement. "It is. You have your license with you?"

Brett reached into the back pocket of his shorts, took out his wallet and eased out the colorful, credit-card-style fishing license. He handed it to the game warden, who reviewed it and said, "Looks like we're all good. You plan on anchoring here overnight?"

"We do. Just taking a few days off," he said.

The warden narrowed his gaze, peered around the boat and noticed the shotgun by the cockpit door. It had him laying a hand on the weapon on his belt as he said, "Do you have a license for that?"

Brett nodded and pulled out both his concealed carry license and an SBS business card, still damp from the unexpected swim he'd taken earlier that day. He handed them to the warden.

"SBS agent, huh? On the job?" the warden asked and returned the documents.

Shaking his head, Brett said, "Just a few days off from work. Shotgun is for protection. I know this area is pretty safe, but I don't like taking chances."

Seemingly satisfied, the other man did a little wave and said, "Enjoy the snapper. My wife makes it oreganata-style and it's delicious."

The other man hopped onto the gunwales and then across into the Boston Whaler. As his partner, a blonde warden, started up the engines and pulled away, the man hauled in the big white bumpers and waved again.

Brett breathed a sigh of relief, picked up the snapper and removed the hook.

Anita popped out from below, walked over to him and, with

a laugh, said, "His wife is right. Oreganata-style would be a good way to cook this."

With a chuckle, Brett nodded. "I'll get it scaled and clean. Do you want me to filet it?" he asked.

"If you don't mind. I'm going to cook up some sides," she said, then turned and went back below.

On the portside of the boat was a bait prep station with a freshwater hose and an assortment of knives and pliers he could use to prepare the filets. Jake had clearly spared no expense when he had equipped his boat.

As he tossed the scales, bones and scraps into the water, an assortment of fish came up to feed. At one point a small blacktip shark swam by to eat the scraps and one of the smaller fish.

The circle of life, Brett thought.

It had him looking back toward the cockpit and wondering about his life.

Anita had never responded to his less-than-subtle probing about meeting her family, but then again, what did he expect?

He wasn't the man she had fallen in love with nearly a decade earlier. The man who had ghosted her because he had lost faith in himself.

But Trey and this assignment had forced him to believe in himself. To trust his gut to do what was right.

And what was right was to finally admit that he still loved her. That he could be the man for her.

If she wanted him, that was. If she was willing to let him into her very busy life. A life she'd worked so hard to build for herself.

But he could handle that. Handle giving her the space she needed because he would need space at times as well if he was going to be a reliable SBS K-9 agent.

Armed with that, he scooped up the filets and whistled to Mango to follow him below.

IT HAD TAKEN Anita some time to familiarize herself with the galley kitchen tucked amidships in the bow, almost directly in front of the cockpit area.

There was one small electric burner and a combo toaster/microwave oven. Beneath them, the fridge was gratefully chilling now that they'd set up the solar panels. To the side was a circular sink and faucet. She'd been careful when using the water, unsure of just how much the boat stored for cooking and washing. But they also had the bottled water just in case.

In the deeper, V-shaped portion of the bow, a comfy-looking padded bench wrapped around the area with a trapezium-shaped table at the center. She hadn't seen any kind of sleeping area except for a small nook to one side. She assumed the table and cushions would do double duty later that night.

The snapper was baking, as the warden had suggested, in the oven. Brett had brought it down earlier but then gone back up to clean up and secure the fishing equipment.

The flavorful aromas of toasty breadcrumbs, garlic and lemon with the subtler sweeter scents of the snapper filled the bow as she stirred a pseudo rice pilaf, a mix of butter, garlic, onion and chicken broth. She had lacked the orzo to make it a real pilaf.

Already resting on the dining table was a plate of roasted asparagus dressed with a simple vinaigrette.

Simple being the key because of the minimal ingredients onboard and the single burner.

It was a real challenge to her normal cooking style, but maybe that was a good thing.

Sometimes she got too caught up in fancy and forgot what was really important.

Like tasty meals made from simple ingredients.

Brett poked his head through the cockpit door. "Permission to come down, Captain," he teased.

She laughed and waved him in. "Permission granted."

It was a tight squeeze past her into the table area as he came down the spiral steps from above, Mango awkwardly hopping from one step to the other. Once he was there, he lifted the cushions to check what was beneath them.

He came up with a bottle of wine that he waggled in the air. "I assume white? Jake has a nice stash in there. Sheets and pillows, too."

"White would be nice," she said, and he tucked it into the fridge.

"Hopefully it will cool down a little," he said, then came up behind her and laid a hand on her waist as he watched her cook.

It was a familiar stance. He'd done it often when they'd been together, always seemingly fascinated by how she created while at the stove.

"Smells good. Looks great," he said. He dropped a kiss on the side of her face and then worked on feeding Mango, spilling out kibble and fresh water into the bowls they'd brought with them.

After, and with nothing to do, he sat at the table and Mango settled at his feet, content now that she'd been fed.

With a side-eyed glance, Anita watched him turn on the burner phone. His fingers flew over the keys and then stilled. His gaze narrowed and his lips thinned into a knife-sharp slash. Another flurry of texting followed until he stopped and powered down the phone again.

"Nothing new?" she asked and stirred, worried about what he might say.

"Police and FBI are still working out the details of the trap. We'll know more in the morning."

The morning. Nearly a dozen hours away, she thought and peered out through the small oval window. Dusk had arrived and night would come quickly, before six at this time of year.

A lot of time for them to be alone together in that confined area.

Memories of the night before flamed to life. She couldn't deny wanting that. Wanting him, but once again she told herself that passion alone wasn't enough.

Because of that, as she stirred the pilaf, she shot him a half glance and said, "It might be nice if you met my parents and sister. *Papi* might be a little gruff. He probably still remembers how you broke my heart."

"I didn't want to," he said, his tone soft, almost pained. "I didn't think you'd want to be with me the way I was."

"I know," she said, then grabbed plates from one of the cubbyholes above the stove and spooned pilaf onto them.

She grabbed pot holders and opened the oven. Satisfied the snapper was ready, she pulled out the pan onto a trivet on the granite countertop. With a long spatula, she lifted the snapper from the pan and laid a filet on each plate beside the pilaf.

She took a few steps to the table, placed a dish before Brett and sat opposite him.

He thanked her, rose and went to the fridge, where he grabbed the wine, twisted off the cap and served it.

His pour was substantially smaller, she realized as he returned with the glasses.

At her questioning glance, he said, "I feel like celebrating, but have to stay sharp."

Smiling, she lifted her glass, and he did the same as she toasted with, "To the tarpon catch, which my dad wouldn't believe without your photo, the snapper and, more importantly, being alive."

He added, "And second chances."

She couldn't disagree. Nodding, she clinked her glass against his and said, "To second chances."

Dinner passed without much talk, both of them seemingly lost in their thoughts and the scrumptious food.

"This is absolutely delicious," he said as he forked up the

last bits of his fish and rice, leaving such a clean plate it didn't seem to need any washing.

Humbled by his praise, she said, "Or maybe you're hungry because we haven't eaten in hours."

He pointed his index finger down at the plate. "No way. This gets five out of five stars in the Madison review of restaurants," he teased.

The heat of a flush swept across her cheeks. "High praise. Thank you," she said, then rose and grabbed her plate, but he stayed her hand.

"You cooked so I'll clean. Why don't you grab another glass of wine and get some fresh air on the foredeck?" he said as he piled all the plates together.

It had been getting a little warm belowdecks. "Will you join me?" she asked, her emotions in turmoil.

She wanted to explore what was happening with him especially since no matter what Brett said, this might be the only time they'd have to be together.

She didn't want to die without experiencing his loving once again.

Chapter Twenty-Seven

Brett nodded. "I won't be long."

He waited until she climbed the tiny, twisty stairs up into the cockpit area. Seconds later he heard her footfall above him as her shadow passed by the porthole in the middle of the ceiling and she settled into the cushions above the bow.

Knowing the clock was ticking between them in so many ways, he hurried in cleaning and drying the dinnerware, pots and pans, and making sure everything was shipshape. Satisfied, he headed above deck, signaling Mango to follow him up.

Anita was lying across the cushions on one side of the foredeck, her head resting along the edge of the gunwale, her gaze focused on the stars that had flared to life with the coming of night.

They weren't all that far from civilization but remote enough that there was little light pollution, making the celestial bodies brilliant against the inky night sky since the moon hadn't risen yet.

He mimicked her posture, stretching out as best he could against the cushions, his long legs hanging over at the end of them. With a click of his tongue, he instructed Mango to lie down and she immediately settled in the middle of the deck.

Gesturing with his hand up at the night sky, he said, "That's Jupiter. The big one."

"Is that Orion over there?" Anita asked, pointing to the telltale belt of three stars that identified that constellation.

"It is," he said, but then silence reigned as they enjoyed the cooler night air and quiet.

There was little movement on the water where they had moored, the boat remaining fairly still on the surface.

He'd left only one small lamp on in the deck below to conserve their power and it cast muted light up through the porthole. But with no moonlight for hours, he had to snap on more lights to warn other boats of their position.

Returning to the cockpit area, he searched beneath the cushions and dug out an anchor light that he snapped into place at the stern and turned on. It cast a glow all around, alerting others to stay clear.

"Bright," Anita said as she came up behind him and stroked a hand down his back.

"Safety," he said and dipped his head in the direction of the cockpit door. "Why don't you head belowdecks. I'll take care of Mango and be down in a second."

She nodded and walked away.

Mango must have followed her aft and now sat at his feet, looking up at him almost accusingly.

Did Mango have a clue what he wanted to do with Anita once they were belowdecks?

"Don't give me that look," he muttered, then grabbed a fresh plastic bag and paper towels from beneath a cushion and set them up at one corner of the stern.

"Hovno," he commanded and pointed at the bag and towels.

Mango hesitated, worrying him. He needed Mango to listen to his commands without fail if they were going to protect Anita.

He repeated the instruction with more urgency, and to his relief, Mango immediately complied. Cleaning up the waste, he stuffed it into a garbage bag beneath one of the cushions and headed to the door of the cockpit.

Mango followed but he raised his hand, palm open and outward, to stop the pit bull.

"Pozor," he said, and without delay, Mango settled herself across the width of the opening.

"Good girl," he said and rubbed her head and fed her a treat.

Closing the cockpit door, he carefully navigated the steps down in the near dark.

Anita had figured out how to convert the dining area for sleeping. Cushions now ran from one side of the bow to the other and she had spread out sheets and pillows on them. She had also opened the four small oval windows and the porthole above, letting the cooler night air sweep through where she lay in the middle of the makeshift bed.

But there was also a narrow sleeping nook to one side of the galley. He flipped a hand in its direction. "I can bunk there if you want."

THIS WAS THE MOMENT, Anita thought.

"I don't want. I want you here. With me," she said, then lay down on the cushions and pulled off her cotton nightshirt, baring her body to him.

He jerked his shirt over his head and tossed it aside. Then he kicked off his boat shoes and hopped around as he slipped off his shorts and briefs before crawling onto the bed with her.

The space was narrow, not that they needed space as they spooned together and made love like there had never been any hurt in the past, but also like they weren't sure of any joy for the future.

He worshipped her with his mouth and hands, exploring every inch of her until she was shaking and pleading with him to take her.

Leaving only long enough to grab a condom and roll it on, he laid a knee on the cushion and, like a big cat, prowled over and slipped between her thighs. But he hesitated and in the dim light of the cabin, it was almost impossible to see his face.

She rose on an elbow, needing to see his face. Needing to know what he was feeling at that exact moment.

She knew even before he said the words.

"I love you, Anita. I've never stopped loving you," he said and cradled her cheek.

"I love you, too, Brett. I loved the man you were, but I love the man you've become even more."

She kissed him, taking his groan of relief deep inside. Taking him deep into her body as he began the rhythm of their loving. He shifted over and over, dropping kisses on her lips and body as he moved, lifting her ever higher until she could no longer refuse giving him everything.

ANITA ARCHED BENEATH HIM, driving him ever deeper, and he lost it.

A harsh breath left him as he climaxed, but he didn't move, riding the wave of their mutual release as long as he could. Even then, he gently lowered himself to her side and laid an arm around her waist.

"I love you," he said again, just to be sure she had no doubt about it.

"I know," she teased, then ran her hand across his arm and turned to face him. The smile on her face was bright even in the murkiness of the night.

"I love you, too," she said.

A sharp breeze swept through the cabin, rousing goose bumps on her skin and making her shiver. He used that opportunity to ease a sheet over her and excuse himself to clean up in the head just off the galley.

When he returned, she had closed her eyes, but sleepily opened them and smiled again before sadness crept into her gaze, turning the green so deep it looked black.

She didn't have to say why. "Don't worry about tomorrow. No matter what, Mango and I will protect you."

"But at what cost?" she said in a strangled voice and laid a hand over his heart. Then she skimmed that hand over the bandages on his chest and the older, scattered shrapnel scars.

He covered his hand with hers and brought it back over his heart. "After what happened, I sometimes felt I didn't deserve to live. I even sometimes didn't care whether I lived or died, but I care now. A lot. There's nothing I won't do so we can be together."

She shifted closer and twined their legs together. Kissing him, she said, "That's what worries me. I want to be safe, but I want you to be safe, too."

He raked back a lock of her hair that had fallen forward. "Trust me," he said, and as she leaned forward to kiss him again, relaxed her body into his, he realized that she did.

She trusted him with her body. With her heart. With her life.

He would guard all three with everything he had no matter what tomorrow brought.

Chapter Twenty-Eight

They woke well before the sun had risen and made love again.

She cooked breakfast just as the first rays of sun, a blurry blend of pinks and purples, filtered through the windows.

They ate and since the tide was so far out, Brett slung Mango over his shoulders so they could walk to a small nearby cay and let Mango relieve herself and run loose. Brett found a piece of driftwood and played fetch with the pit for well over half an hour, exercising her after the day spent cooped up on the boat.

Soon, however, the tide started coming in and reality drifted in with it, she thought.

Brett scooped up Mango again, struggling slightly with the pit bull's weight and the deeper water. Mango seemed skittish, probably recalling what had happened the day before.

Fortunately, they were able to board Jake's boat without any problems.

But once onboard, Anita felt like a caged animal, anxiously awaiting the moment when Trey would call.

Like her, Brett nervously paced back and forth across the stern, constantly checking his watch.

The sun rose, bringing heat in the early morning.

She sat beneath the canopy protecting the console area, trying to stay cool. Telling herself the damp sweat across her body was from the ever-rising temperature and not fear.

It seemed like hours and yet it had barely been twenty minutes since they'd come onboard. Brett powered up the phone and it rang.

"Any progress?" he asked, put the phone on speaker and walked back to where she sat.

"Police and FBI have a plan. They want you to come to the Miami Beach Marina on Alton Road," Trey said, and it was obvious from his tone that he was less than happy with the plan.

"That's a busy marina," Brett said, apparently well familiar with it.

"It is, but they're making arrangements for you to come into the slips by the watersports and parasailing companies," he said.

"That's a pretty exposed area. There's the causeway and at least two parking lots nearby. Perfect spots for a shooter," Brett countered.

"It is, which is why we're working up our own plan to protect you. Do you have your laptop?" Trey asked.

"I do. I should be able to use this phone as a hot spot," he advised, worry about the plan overriding concerns about someone tracking the phone.

"Law enforcement wants you at the dock at thirteen hundred, but I think we have enough time to have a meeting," Trey responded, and from the background, someone called out to him.

"We do have time. It should only take a little over two hours to get there," Brett advised.

"Roger. Give us an hour at most," Trey said and ended the call.

She'd been staring back and forth from the phone to Brett's face, trying to read what he was thinking and feeling.

"You're really worried," she said because it was so obvious from the deep ridges across his forehead and the frown lines bracketing his mouth.

He nodded and ran a hand across the short strands of hair

at the top of his head. "Like I told Trey, that area is really exposed. We'd be close to a walkway along the edge of the marina. Anyone could take potshots at us from the causeway or parking lots and then hop into a car and speed off."

She stroked a hand across his arm, trying to reassure him. "What can *we* do?"

BRETT'S MIND HAD been running through possibilities as Trey had been speaking, imagining the area at the marina that he knew quite well.

When he had first arrived in Miami so many months earlier, he had used to rent WaveRunners there before he had reconnected with Jake and visited him down on Key Largo instead.

"Let me show you the area so you're familiar with it," he said and hopped down the stairs belowdecks to where he'd stowed his things.

He pulled out his laptop and went back on deck. He placed the computer on the free space of the passenger console, powered it up and turned on the phone's hot spot. It took a few seconds for the laptop to connect to the wireless, but as soon as it did, he pulled up a satellite view of the area to show Anita the layout of the marina and the nearby elements.

Running his fingers along the screen, he pointed out the areas he thought would be the riskiest. "If I pull in here, you'll be exposed. Anyone in these parking lots or the causeway will have a shot and easy escape."

ANITA TRACKED BRETT'S FINGER, understanding his concerns. Unless he reversed the boat into a slip, a possibly time-consuming maneuver, she'd be a sitting duck if she was above board.

"Someone can shoot at me from all these areas," she said, motioning to the locations with her index finger.

"Nothing about Kennedy says *sniper*, so I'd rule out the far parking lot. Causeway is possibly too exposed. There's nowhere to hide," Brett advised, but then quickly tacked on, "My money is on that walkway and the ground level of that parking lot."

She agreed, which made her say, "I think you're right. I could hide belowdecks, but if I do—"

"We might not draw him out. He's not likely to shoot at you once you're surrounded by the police and FBI. He wants to do it before," he said and waggled his head, obviously unsettled.

"I have to be where he can see me," she said, willing to take the risk if it would bring an end to the nightmare.

He encircled her shoulder with his hand and drew her close. "I don't want you hurt. There has to be another way."

She shook her head and laughed harshly. "I could wear a disguise. Maybe one of those fake noses with the glasses and moustache," she kidded.

Brett's eyes opened wide, and she could swear she saw the light bulb pop up over his head.

"It's not a bad idea."

It HAD TAKEN him almost all night and multiple calls to reach his informant at the FBI.

He had worried that the man wouldn't come through for him, but he had finally answered as Santiago had been picking up a *café con leche* and Cuban toast at a small breakfast shop in a strip mall not far from Jake's home.

"*Mano*, why are you avoiding me?" he asked, trying for a friendly tone and not the worry twisting his gut into knots.

In a low whisper, the man said, "Things are moving quickly here. They plan on bringing the woman in today."

"Where?" he asked and sipped on the coffee, wincing as the heat of it burned his tongue.

His informant hesitated, making Santiago worry that the man was going to burn him as well, but then he said, "I need to know this is it. If I give you this info—"

"You're paid in full," he said, because if he didn't finish this woman and maybe Marino as well, Hollywood was going to finish him.

"They're on a boat and coming into the Miami Beach Marina," the FBI agent said and continued laying out the details of the plan for bringing in the chef and the SBS agent.

Santiago listened carefully, logging all the info into his brain while planning what he would do at the same time.

After the man hung up, he considered what he'd heard and finalized his plan.

Surprise, firepower and speed.

That would be the key to ending this disaster.

BRETT NAVIGATED PAST Key Biscayne, steering toward the Bay Bridge in the Rickenbacker Causeway. Once he cleared the bridge, he'd head toward Fisher Island and work his way into the Government Cut to reach the marina just as planned.

The boat's radio crackled, snapping to life, and Trey's voice erupted across the line. "We're in place," he said.

"Roger that. We're on schedule. Any luck with the search warrant at Kennedy's place?" Trey had mentioned in an earlier call that a judge had finally felt they had enough evidence thanks to the DNA match from the blood at the Homestead location.

"Police executed the warrant this morning. His mom wasn't surprised that the police were knocking on her door. We expect them to bring us some of his clothing in about twenty minutes so we can confirm it's him," Trey said.

Brett bit back a curse. "That's cutting it close, *mano*."

"I know, *mano*. I know," Trey said wearily.

"I'll radio as soon as I'm closer," he said and replaced the handset on the console hook.

He thrust forward, catching sight of the luxury buildings

on Fisher Island and the ferry that carried residents to the ex-clusive enclave.

Slowing, he made sure he was clear of any other boats or the large ocean cruise ships that also used the man-made chan-nel. Satisfied the way was clear, he gunned the engine, aware they had a schedule to keep.

Heart pounding, hands gripping the steering wheel so tightly they cramped, he searched the area, keen eyes taking in the boats parked in the marina slips. Everything from immense multimillion-dollar cabin cruisers to small fishing boats. Peo-ple walked here and there on the docks, worrying him.

Kennedy could be one of those people as well.

As he passed the last few docks for the marina, he throttled down the engine and radioed Trey. "I'm here. Heading toward the watersports dock."

"Roger. Matt and Natalie have the sample. They're search-ing the ground floor of that parking lot right now."

Little consolation, Brett thought. It might be way too late already.

They would be sitting ducks as he pulled into the slip, es-pecially since the police and FBI agents would not jump into action until they had a clear view of Kennedy.

If he even decided to show up.

But Wilson's program had predicted he would, and Trey had reached out to his psychologist brother, Ricky, whose pro-file of Kennedy warned he was a loose cannon and probably fearless of what might happen to him. Ricky had agreed with Wilson's program.

Brett couldn't disagree. Anyone who would knowingly take out Hollywood's nephew, and his own cousin, was reckless.

But that kind of reckless came with a price.

He hoped one of the many agents supposedly stationed in and around the marina would be able to either take him down or take him into custody.

Turning to the starboard side, he navigated into the gap for the last slips next to the floating docks for the WaveRunners and other personal watercraft.

This is it. This is when it'll happen, he thought and risked a quick last glance at the console seat opposite him.

Chapter Twenty-Nine

As he turned starboard again, motion on the walkway caught his attention.

Kennedy in full body armor. Agents racing from all over, but all too far to make a difference.

Bullets sprayed across the side of the boat, shattering the windscreen and pinging against the metal railings and hull.

Brett released the wheel and hit the deck, swiping the throttle on the way down to kill the engine.

A surprising pause came in the shooting. Metal clacking was followed by a loud stream of Spanish curses.

Brett jumped to his feet, pointed at land and shouted, *"Vpred. Útok."*

Mango leaped from the boat and at Kennedy, a white-and-tan missile flying through the air.

To protect her, Brett fired at the other man, who seemed to be struggling with the magazine on the assault rifle.

The bullet struck his shoulder, and he staggered back.

Mango latched onto his right arm and thrashed her head until he dropped the weapon.

Kennedy was screaming and trying to dislodge the pit bull as Brett leaped from the boat, ran down the dock and launched himself at Kennedy, tackling him to the ground.

"Pust, Mango. *Pust*," he said so the dog would release his hold.

Mango instantly complied and Brett flipped Kennedy onto

his stomach and placed a knee in the middle of his back to hold him down as an assortment of agents swarmed around them, including Trey and his fellow K-9 agents, Matt and Natalie.

Trey helped him to his feet, but as he looked toward the boat, he cursed. "Anita. *Dios*, Anita," he said and was about to race to the dock when Brett laid a hand on his arm.

"It's okay, Trey," he said and faced the boat where Anita slumped on the console seat.

"What do you mean it's okay?" Trey shouted, almost frantic.

"Anita, you can come out now," Brett called out and headed back onto the boat to help Anita from belowdecks.

Trey hurried over with the other SBS K-9 agents as well as several other SBS personnel, local law enforcement and some suits he assumed were the Feds.

ANITA SHAKILY CLIMBED the stairs to the deck, heart hammering and a sick feeling in her gut, especially as she looked at "herself" on the console seat.

A number of bullets had torn through the dummy they had assembled in secret.

Fake Anita had been fashioned from some boat cushions, Anita's clothes and handfuls of dry seaweed ribbons Brett had gathered that morning to make fake hair held in place by a baseball cap. Foam guts spilled from the body, a reminder of how deadly the shots might have been if she had been sitting there.

She quickly examined Brett, who had been exposed to the gunfire, shifting her hands across his chest and arms as she searched for any injuries.

He grasped her hands and held them tenderly. "I'm okay."

"Mango?" she said and peered toward the dock where the pit bull sat beside her K-9 counterparts, tongue hanging from her mouth. Not a scratch on her apparently.

Relief washed through her, making her knees weak.

As she started to crumple, Brett hugged an arm around her waist and offered support.

She glanced up at him and smiled. "Thanks."

"Ms. Reyes," said one of the suits as he dipped his head in greeting and approached the boat. "I'm Special Agent Santoro. We'd like to have a word with you."

"She's not going anywhere without me," Brett said.

The FBI agent hesitated, but recognizing that Brett was serious, he said, "If you both wouldn't mind coming with us to the police station." He gestured to the dock, inviting them to deboard and follow him.

Trey laid a hand on her shoulder. "I'll have Aunt Elena meet you there in case you need assistance."

"Thanks, Trey," Brett said and glanced at her intently. "Are you ready to go?"

Anita nodded and accepted the FBI agent's assistance onto the dock. But once she was there, she turned and examined the beautiful new boat, now pockmarked with ugly bullet holes. The windscreen lay in ruined shards on the deck. A side window had also been blown out.

She glanced at Brett and then at Trey. "I think you owe your friend a new boat."

WHEN THEY ARRIVED at the Miami Beach police station, Detective Williams was waiting there along with Roni and Trey's aunt, a respected trial attorney. Tia Elena had married Trey's father's brother. Tio Jose was a member of the Miami district attorney's office and the man who had helped them negotiate the plea deal with the crooked cop.

They greeted Roni effusively, happy to see her. "Isn't it too soon after the baby?" Brett asked, worried that she was pushing herself before she was ready.

Roni smiled, a tired smile that spoke volumes about the demands of tending to a newborn. "I'm just here for the interview and the lineup. I had to be here for that," she said.

Brett understood. It was a huge collar to not only get Kennedy but also possibly a mobster like Tony Hollywood.

Special Agent Santoro had been waiting patiently as they exchanged niceties, but clearly wasn't happy with the delay and the presence of Elena Gonzalez.

As Trey's aunt introduced herself to the FBI agent, he said, "There's really no reason for you to be here. Ms. Reyes isn't a suspect."

Elena nodded. "I know, but we want to make sure everything is done properly so that both Kennedy and Hollywood don't have any cracks to crawl through. Ms. Reyes needs closure so she can get on with her life."

Brett had been standing next to Anita, a hand on her shoulder, offering support. She jumped with Elena's words and softly said, "I need to get on with my life."

After she said that, she shot a quick look up in his direction and smiled, offering hope that her life would be one spent with him.

Agent Santoro's lips thinned into a line of displeasure. "Let's get going, then."

They walked toward one of the police interrogation rooms, but when they reached it, the FBI agent barred his entry with a beefy arm.

"You'll have to wait outside," he said and then eyeballed Roni and Williams. "I assume you two will tape this for us?"

"We'll be in the viewing room. Brett can join us there," Roni said and directed him to a door several feet away from the interrogation room.

He walked with Roni and her partner to the viewing room and was about to enter when he turned and locked his gaze with Anita's. He mouthed, "You'll be fine."

She offered him a weak smile, nodded and entered the room.

WHAT SEEMED LIKE hours dragged by as she answered questions for Santoro and his partner, who had walked into the interrogation room right after Trey's tia Elena and she had entered.

She was grateful for Elena, whose steady presence and gentle encouragement buoyed her flagging energy and patience. She wanted all this over. She wanted to get back to her restaurant. She wanted to get back to Brett.

When the interrogation finished, they took her to another room with a large two-way mirror that faced a narrow space. A lineup room, she realized from the true crime shows she watched. The far wall of that space had horizontal lines that marked off the height of the men who marched into the room.

"I'll be waiting outside," Elena said and squeezed Anita's shoulder in reassurance.

The door closed behind Elena, leaving her alone with Agent Santoro. A few seconds later, six men walked into the lineup room. They were all dressed similarly and of like height, race and weight. Once they were in the room, Santoro had them step to the left and then to the right before facing forward again.

"Can you identify the man who shot Manuel Ramirez? Take your time," he said.

Because of his admonition, Anita examined each man carefully even though she had recognized Kennedy right away. Slowly drifting her gaze over each face, she finally said, "It's the third man from the left. That's the man I saw that night."

"Are you sure?" Santoro asked.

Anita nodded. "I'm sure."

With a wave of his hand, Santoro directed her out of the room. Not only was Elena there, but she had also been joined by Roni, Williams and Brett.

She immediately went to Brett's side and slipped her hands into his. "I'm ready to go."

Turning, she looked at the FBI agent and said, "Are we done now?"

Santoro peered at her and then Roni and Williams. "We're done…for now. We may have more questions for you."

Relief swept through her until Roni asked, "What about Hollywood? When do we pull him in?"

Agent Santoro clearly didn't like being challenged by Roni. "As soon as *we* finish with Kennedy. His lawyer has already offered to flip on Hollywood to avoid the death penalty," he said, his tone as biting as a great white shark.

Roni wasn't backing down. She walked up to the much taller and broader agent and rose up on her tiptoes until she was almost nose to nose with him. "You button this up and keep Anita out of Hollywood's business. She has nothing to do with that."

She appreciated Roni's defense, worried that this wouldn't be over if Hollywood thought she was a threat to his freedom in any way.

"I got it, Detective. Your friend doesn't need to worry about Hollywood or Kennedy," Santoro said.

Brett slipped an arm around her waist and said, "We'll get going, then. I'm sure Anita wants to check in with her restaurant and her parents, and get some rest."

At Santoro's nod, she thanked Elena for her help and hugged Roni, embracing the other woman hard since she imagined it had taken a lot for her to leave her newborn to come to the station. She shook hands with Williams, Santoro and his partner, and then Brett was there again, his arm around her waist as he guided her out of the station and out to the large plaza in front of the building.

The FBI agents had driven them to the station in one of their vehicles, but it would be an easy enough walk to her restaurant and then her condo, although her things, including her pocketbook and keys, were still on the boat.

"What now?" she asked, looking around and wondering what to do about so many things.

He cradled her cheek and smiled wistfully. "What do you want to do now?"

Pushing away a lock of hair that had come loose of her top-knot, she shook her head, confused about almost everything except one thing.

"I want to be with you. I love you, Brett. I want a life with you."

His smile broadened and he wrapped his arms around her waist and drew her close for a deep kiss.

When they finally broke apart, he said, "I love you, too, Anita. I want a life with you, too, but there's one thing I want right now."

Puzzled, she narrowed her gaze, wondering what it was, especially seeing the gleam in his dark eyes, so reminiscent of the young man she had fallen in love with so many years earlier.

"What is that?" she asked.

He spread the fingers of one hand wide across his stomach and, with a broad smile on his face, said, "A nice big bowl of your famous chicken and rice. With chorizo this time. Do you think you can do that?"

She stopped, faced him and cupped his face in her hands. Rising on her tiptoes, she brushed a kiss on his lips and said, "I can do that today and forever."

He chuckled. "I might get a little tired of chicken and rice forever, but I'll never get tired of you," he said and deepened the kiss until a rough cough broke them apart.

Trey was standing there holding her pocketbook and a set of car keys, which he handed to Brett.

Eyeballing them, he said, "I guess things are good between you two?"

Brett smiled and said, "Never been better."

He tugged her hand, leading her in the direction of the SBS SUV sitting at the curb, and as she hurried there with him, eager to get to her restaurant and the after, she couldn't argue with him.

They'd faced death multiple times and now it was time to live, Brett at her side. Forever. Nothing could ever be better than that.

* * * * *

If you missed the previous books in New York Times *bestselling author Caridad Piñeiro's miniseries, South Beach Security: K-9 Division, look for:*

Sabotage Operation
Escape the Everglades
Killer in the Kennel

Available now wherever Harlequin Intrigue books are sold!